VIOLET SERENADE

Violet Serenade

Book 5

L.A. REMENICKY

Lavish
Publishing LLC

Contents

First Edition

Fairfield Corners Series Book 5

All Rights Reserved

Published in the United States by Lavish Publishing, LLC, Midland, Texas

Paperback Edition

ISBN: 9781944985288

Cover Design by: Victor R. Sosa

Cover Images: Adobe Stock

www.LavishPublishing.com

Chapter One

Seven Years Ago...

VIOLET

Violet stifled a giggle as Dane pulled her down the stairs, careful to miss the squeaky spots.

"Shhh… you want your dad to hear us?" he whispered.

She put her hand over her mouth to muffle any sound. No way did she want Dane to get in trouble, he did enough of that on his own.

Once they were out on the porch and the door was closed, he turned to her and dangled the keys from his fingers. "I thought we could go out to the Island."

The Island was a peninsula on the shoreline of Little Beaver Lake, popular with Fairfield Corners' fishermen. The Island was *the* spot for parties, and high school kids had been partying out there for generations.

Shocked, she tried to pull her hand out of his. "Dad's going to rip you a new one if you get caught with mom's car without permission."

"Don't worry about it, I just want to spend some time alone with you. You trust me, right?"

Yes, she trusted him. They'd been best friends since the day he came to them as a scared seven-year-old. He was the first of many foster children that called Cassie and Logan Miller's house their home over the years. He was the only one who hadn't moved on to getting adopted or gone back to their biological parents. Cassie once asked him if he wanted them to adopt him. He'd shaken his head no before running off to find Violet.

Vi climbed into the car and scooted over to the middle of the front seat to be as close to Dane as possible.

"Nope. Scoot over and buckle up."

"You big worry wart, nothing's gonna happen."

"Doesn't matter, scoot. This car does not move until you're buckled in."

She stuck her tongue out at him but complied. Practically vibrating with nervous energy, she tapped her fingers on the armrest in time to a song only she could hear. She'd always loved Dane, but her feelings had started to change as she grew up. They grew stronger and deeper than mere friendship, into the love between a man and a woman. She hoped that's what he wanted to talk to her about at the Island because she was ready to tell him how her feelings had changed.

Once they were down the street and away from the house, he lowered the windows and turned on the radio, letting the warm night air rush through the car as he drove toward the lake.

Dane

He stared at the road in front of them, trying to figure out how he was going to explain to Vi that he was leaving tomorrow for boot camp. It would be the first time they would be apart for more than a day or two.

He'd loved her since that first day when those deep blue eyes of hers had looked deep into his soul and accepted him for who he was. She said something about his music being all black and swirly, and that was it for him. They'd been best friends since that day, but now he knew he had to leave her behind, at least for a while. It was going to hurt—a lot—but it had to be done. No matter how much he loved her, he'd made a promise.

He was eighteen and high school graduation was behind him. His grades weren't good enough for college, leaving him very few choices. A manufacturing job sounded way too boring and the service industry... Well, just the thought of it made him shudder. That left trade school or military service. Traveling the world sounded more like him than some boring job, so that's what he decided. The previous month he'd asked Logan to take him to the recruiting office in Fort Wayne. After checking all his options, he decided to enlist in the Army.

His only problem now was telling Vi. Just the thought of leaving her behind in Fairfield Corners made him want to puke, but it had to be done. He had to make his way in the world, and the military was his only option. He'd put off telling her, trying to find the perfect moment which never came. It was the day before he was to leave for boot camp and he was panicking, he hadn't told her he was leaving. Just the thought of making her sad made it hard for him to breathe. He would do anything for her, but he'd made a promise to Logan.

After their visit to the recruiter, Logan had taken him to the drive-in diner. As they waited for their food, Logan had asked Dane how he felt about Vi.

"So, Dane, I know you and Vivi are really close."

"Yes, sir." He picked at the hole in the knee of his jeans. "I..." he stumbled over his words. "You know we've been friends since that first day. She helped me see that I was worth something, worth more than what my dad did to Bette."

"I'm glad she was there for you. Cassie and I were clueless about how to help you come to terms with what happened."

"We've been best friends for so long, I was surprised when I realized my feelings for her outgrew mere friendship."

The carhop walked up with the tray of food and drinks.

Finally, something to ease the dryness in my throat. After a big slurp of soda, Dane swallowed hard, better just get it over with. "I love her," he blurted out.

Logan coughed. "You what?"

Saying it the second time was easier. "I love her. I know she's too young, but I can't help how I feel."

Logan took a bite of his burger and chewed thoughtfully.

"Are you mad?"

"No, but I am worried."

Dane's face paled and he felt like he was going to puke up what he'd just eaten. "Worried? That I'll hurt her? That I'm like my dad?"

"God, no. That's not it at all. I didn't mean for you to feel like…" He rubbed his chin. "Shit, I knew I was going to screw this up."

Dane looked at his burger but couldn't make himself take a bite. He was afraid it would choke him.

"What I meant was she's so young, only fourteen. I want her to experience everything about being a kid. Dates and parties and dances. I'm afraid she'll skip all that if you two become too close too fast. I don't want her to feel like she missed out on anything. Do you understand what I'm saying?"

"Sort of."

"Basically, I want you to promise me you'll let her grow up and discover who she is when she isn't half of the Violet and Dane duo."

His heart thundered in his chest. *God, why is this so hard?* The words stuck in his throat; he wasn't sure what Logan was asking him to promise. "So, what does that mean, exactly?"

Logan blew out a breath. "I want you to keep your feelings to yourself. She's too young to be committed to a guy, even if it is you."

It would likely kill him, but he'd do it. He'd do anything for his Vi. "Okay, I promise." He drank the rest of his soda and crumpled the wrapper around the remains of his burger as his stomach churned. He wasn't ready to admit to Logan that he didn't want to tell Vi he was leaving.

"You feeling okay? Usually, you plow through two burgers but you didn't even finish one."

"Just not hungry. Nervous about leaving home, I guess."

"Is that all?" Logan asked, concern written all over his face.

"Yeah." As Logan drove toward home, Dane worried about how to tell Vi he was leaving.

Now he was out of time. He was packing his stuff to leave first thing in the morning. Every time he'd tried to tell Vi he was leaving, the words got stuck in his throat. *God, what if she cries?* Her tears gutted him, even when they were from watching a sappy movie. He just couldn't stand to see her cry. Telling her he was leaving was sure to break her heart.

He'd left before dinner, telling Cassie he'd pick up something.

"One last look around?" she'd asked, knowing he was feeling anxious about leaving.

"Yeah. Maybe I'll get a burger or something."

"Be home before ten."

He nodded. "Okay."

He'd wandered aimlessly around the square until most of the businesses had closed up for the night. Even the streets were empty, as if something had picked up all the town's inhabitants and relocated them somewhere else. He kicked at some stones on the sidewalk and checked his watch. Almost ten, he'd better head back home. Vi still didn't know he was leaving. It was a weeknight, so even the teens were home early. Shivering from the cool breeze, he ambled home.

As he climbed the steps, he decided he had to tell her. All the lights were off when he unlocked the front door. Then he decided there was one more thing he wanted to do before he left town—go spend some time over on The Island. That was it! That was where he would tell Vi he was leaving for boot camp in the morning.

He rummaged around in his closet until he found his old backpack. Creeping down to the living room, he stuffed in the throw from the back of the couch and headed for the kitchen. Tucking a couple of bottles of water and a bag of chips on top of the blanket, he started to zip it up but then realized it would be a perfect night for a bonfire. He grabbed a pack of matches off the fireplace mantel and set the backpack by the front door.

Sneaking back up the stairs, he tapped on Vi's door and poked his head into her room. "You awake Vi?"

"Yeah."

He swallowed thickly and convinced her to sneak out of the house with him.

∿

The ride was silent. Thoughts whirled in his mind, wondering if there was a perfect spot to give her the news.

He pulled off the road and into the clearing, his mind full of memories. Staring off into the darkness, he didn't notice Vi had gotten out of the car until she pulled open his door.

"Come on, slow poke. Can we build a fire?"

"Yeah, sure," he replied, glad he'd tucked some matches into the backpack.

They trekked through the trees, stopping when they stepped out onto the beach. The lights from one of the cottages across the lake shone through the dark, highlighting how late it was. God, he hoped they didn't get caught, Logan would have a coronary if he caught them out here alone after dark.

He set the bag down next to the fire ring and walked over to the lean-to to grab a couple of logs for the fire. "You want to get some sticks for kindling?"

"Sure," Vi answered, trotting into the forest to look for dead branches that would light easily.

He stacked the logs as Logan had taught him, crumpling up some newspaper he'd brought specifically for that purpose since he knew Vi loved a campfire. He looked up when she dropped an armload of sticks next to the fire ring.

"Think that's enough?"

"More than enough, we'll leave any extras by the woodpile." The lake residents kept the woodpile stocked.

Dane pulled the blanket out of the backpack and spread it out on the sand close enough to the fire to keep them warm. "Come here, I need to talk to you about something."

She sat on the blanket and scooched over close to him, resting her head on his shoulder. "This is nice."

He worked to keep his breathing even. Having Vi sitting so close made his dick want to come out and play. *Jesus, calm the fuck down, this is Vi and she's only fourteen.*

After kissing the top of her head, he wrapped her in his arms.
Whoop whoop.

"What the…" he muttered as he stood.

Red and blue lights flashed through the trees.

"Shit."

A light shone into his face.

"What the…? Dane? Violet?" Logan bellowed, the flashlight beam going from Dane to Vi and back again.

"You into stealing cars now, son?"

Dane hung his head, "No, sir. I just…"

"Violet, get into my car…now." He watched his daughter shuffle over to the cruiser and get in the front seat, her face angry. "What the actual fuck, Dane? You made me a promise and now I find you out here at the Island alone with her. She's only fourteen!"

"I know, I…"

"We'll talk when we get home. Cassie was worried sick when she realized her car was gone, and so were the two of you." He ran his hands through his hair. "You drive Cassie's car home, and no funny stuff; I'll be right on your bumper. You will apologize to her for taking her car without permission. We will discuss this further when we get home."

The next morning, Logan woke Dane early to leave for his intake into the Army. He hadn't dared to try and sneak into Vi's room with Logan being so pissed.

He stared at the seatback in front of him as the bus lurched forward, taking him to the next part of his life. With no time to talk to Vi, he'd written a letter and put it in their place—behind the loose brick in the fireplace. She'd know to look there.

Chapter Two

Present Day

VIOLET

Thunder rumbled overhead as she sped along the highway, the cornfields rushing by in the gloom of a late summer thunderstorm. It seemed like just yesterday she'd been driving in the opposite direction, headed for Temple University to start her freshman year. And now, four years later, she was headed home for good. Home, where she could be herself instead of pretending to be a carefree student.

Home held so many memories that hadn't faded, not even a little. He'd been gone for seven years, and she *still* cried herself to sleep every night. When he'd left, it had felt like half of her being had been violently stripped away. Everywhere she'd turned there'd been another memory of the time they'd spent together, so she'd been happy to go out of state to get her degree in music therapy. The degree was a promise to her parents, but her real love was performing. Freshman year, she started playing at every open mic night she could find. By her junior year, she was an in-demand act for the local bars. Coming home felt right, even if it did feel a little like giving in. She wanted to make her way in the music industry on her talent alone.

The closer she got to Fairfield Corners, the better she felt—better than she'd felt in seven years. Wow, it was hard to believe it had been that long since he'd been gone. Lost in her thoughts, she hadn't kept an eye on the speedometer and the whoop of a siren behind her had her glancing at it guiltily. *Whoopsie.*

She watched in the rearview mirror as the deputy put on his hat, preparing to step out of his car and into the downpour.

Oh damn, I'm in freakin' Fairfield County! Dad will surely hear about this. She ran her fingers through her hair and swiped at the tears on her cheeks. This was going to be so embarrassing.

She jumped at the tap on the window. Pressing the down button, she looked up at the deputy.

Double damn. It's him. The reason she'd fled her hometown and gone to school two states away was standing outside her car in the pouring rain. But six hundred plus miles couldn't erase the memory of him, or how she'd been completely devastated when he left.

She put on the face she'd perfected over the last four years. To the outside world, she looked normal; happy even. But inside, she was still that fourteen-year-old girl curled up in a ball, wondering what she'd done that was so wrong he up and left without a word.

Looking up, she held on tight to that mask. "Oh, hi Dane." She held out her license and registration, hoping he hadn't noticed her mask slip before she slammed it back into place.

The rain stopped as if on cue, the silence broken by the plop of water dripping from the brim of his hat. He took the proffered items and turned back to his cruiser.

Not even a hello. Guess some things haven't changed. Her mom had told her he was back, but she'd ignored it, hoping he'd leave before she graduated. Why had he come back to Fairfield Corners? As a teen, he'd been all about getting out of the small town. *Maybe coming home wasn't such a good idea after all.*

Cars whizzing past drowned out the sound of his footsteps as he returned to her car.

"Slow down," he growled as he handed her items back to her. "I won't give you a ticket this time, but next time…."

She smiled, her face felt like it would crack into a million pieces. "Thank you, Dane." She watched as his music swirled black and gray, jerking around him. *Wow, he's upset.*

"Your dad's waiting for you at the sheriff's station." He said before turning and going back to his car.

"What crawled up his butt?" She muttered as she watched him pull back onto the highway and disappear down the road towards Fairfield Corners. *You'd think I did something to him instead of the other way around.* After checking for traffic, she took off toward town.

Black clouds were giving way to blue sky when she pulled into the parking lot of the Fairfield County Sheriff's department. Two patrol cars sat in their spaces near the door. She hoped one of them wasn't Dane's.

The smell always hit her first, what she thought of as burnt coffee and testosterone. Then were the sounds, ringing phones and the static of the police band. So many hours spent sitting at an empty desk coloring as her father did the mountain of paperwork that came with the job.

"Violet!"

She turned around to find the sheriff standing there, his arms folded over his chest.

"Uncle James," she cried as she hurried to him, holding out her arms for a hug.

After the warm greeting, he set her back from him and tried to look at her sternly.

She giggled when the corner of his mouth quirked up. "I'm sorry, I know I was speeding but I just wanted to get home."

"Don't lie to me, Vi. You were lost in the music in your head, weren't you?"

"Okay, we'll go with that." No way was she going to admit she'd been thinking about Dane and how he'd left without a word when she should have been paying attention to the road. Besides, she didn't want to admit she hadn't looked at anyone's music for quite some time.

A deep voice growled, "Violet Miller, you better have a good explanation."

She stood on tiptoe to peek over the sheriff's shoulder, her angry father's blue eyes locked with hers. Her gaze drifted to the floor as she mumbled, "I was just in a hurry to get home. I didn't realize…" He'd always been able to look her in the eye and tell if she was lying.

He held out his arms and murmured, "Come here, Vi," then pulled her into a hug.

Ensconced in his arms, she took a deep sniff, inhaling the scent that was uniquely her father—his woodsy cologne mixed with the smell of gun oil.

"I missed you, Daddy."

"I'm glad you're home. Have you been by the store yet?"

She looked up at him. "No. Someone told me you were waiting, so I came here first." She didn't even want to say his name.

He squeezed her tighter, "Let's get you over to your mom before she sends out a search party. Give me five minutes to straighten up my desk."

She let her wall down and snuck a peek at her father's music—it was his normal red and blue swirls, with a few pink streaks. *Phew. He isn't really mad, just worried.*

The most important thing she'd learned at college hadn't been in a classroom, but through plain old trial and error: how to block out everyone's music. She saw music swirling around everyone, and its colors told her more about that person than their facial expressions ever would. Their music couldn't be manipulated so it was always true. The sheer number of people she came in contact with on a daily basis put her in crisis mode. The sensory overload almost had her running back home after the first week. Slowly, she taught herself how to ignore the music by pushing it into the background. She could often go days without slipping, but now she'd slipped up twice in one day.

Her dad pulled open the door and ushered her inside the store. She stopped and let the atmosphere of the space wash over her until she heard her name.

"Violet Miller, come over here and give your Aunt Janet a hug. I can't believe you've graduated from college; it seems like it was just yesterday you were toddling around the store and learning to walk."

After a hug she turned to find her mother standing there, a serious expression on her face.

Crap, Dad blabbed. "Hi, Mom," she said as she stepped into her arms. "The store looks great. Did you get the couches recovered? They look amazing!"

"What's this I hear about you speeding?"

"Oh geez, someone has a big mouth," she said with a smile as she looked over at her dad. "When did Dane start working as a deputy? And what's crawled up his ass? He barely said a word to me."

"Language," her mother admonished, ignoring her comment about Dane.

"I know, I know. A lady shouldn't curse. I'll remember that the next time your book order is screwed up."

"Yeah, well, some situations call for a more colorful vocabulary. Now, who wants a drink? We've got some new summer drinks that are yummy."

"No thanks, Mom. I really want to get home, unpack, and take a nice hot bath. I've sure missed that big old claw foot tub."

"Okay, but don't take too long. Everyone is going over to The Pub tonight to celebrate you coming home for good."

The bell over the door jangled and she looked over to find Dane striding into the store. He stopped and stared at her. "Oh, sorry, I thought you were still at the station. I just needed to stop and talk with Bette." He walked toward the connected storefront that housed Bette's Beautiful Things. Vi watched as he studiously ignored her. *Geez, what a dick.*

"You want a cup, Dane?" Cassie asked as he walked past the coffee bar, already pouring his favorite brew into a to-go cup. At his nod, she snapped a lid on the cup and slipped it into a sleeve before handing it to him. "We're having a welcome home party for Violet at The Pub tonight. Are you going to be there?"

"Sorry, I'm on shift until ten." He leaned over and kissed Cassie on the cheek. "Next time." A quick glance in Vi's direction and he was gone.

"See? He won't even look at me." With a sigh, she picked up her purse, "That bathtub is calling me. Six at The Pub?"

"Yes. Go home, relax, I'll see you later."

Cassie watched as her daughter left the store and disappeared. "What is going on with those two? If they don't straighten up, Mama Bear is going to have to wade in—and no one wants that."

Logan laughed. "They're adults, Cass. Give them some time to work through whatever this is."

"But I can tell Violet is upset."

"Give them some room, Mama Bear. They were so close before he left for basic training, I'm sure they'll work it out."

"I hope you're right, Dudley."

The bell over the door tinkled. Cassie looked over to see a delivery guy with a clipboard in his hand. "Hi, Cassie. You want to unlock the back door for me?"

"Sure, just let me grab my keys."

She kissed her husband and headed for her office. "I hope this order is right," she muttered to herself. "Don't want to have to use that colorful vocabulary."

Chapter Three

DANE

He forced his fingers to unclench from around the steering wheel. Seeing her sitting in that car had made his mind whirl and his stomach roil. One glance and those eyes of hers had bored down deep into his soul, dredging up all those old feelings like a swift punch to his gut— ones he thought he'd gotten past long ago.

"Fuck," he muttered as he ran his hands over his face. He'd been a scared, broken, seven-year-old when the Millers took him in as a foster kid. Violet had been sitting on the front steps with her mom, Cassie, when he'd first come to live with them. Without blinking, she'd stood and taken his hand. "I'll show you your new room." So grown up for only being four years old.

Her eyes, an unusual bright blue, had stared at him curiously as he sat on the bed. "Your song is all black and swirly. Why?"

"My song?"

"Yeah, your song. Everyone has a song. Can't you see them?"

"Just go away and leave me alone, would ya?"

"Okay." One last long look, then she was gone. That one look had him squirming under her scrutiny, as if she could see his innermost thoughts. It irritated him, but he surprisingly wanted to protect her.

He still had seven hours left on his shift, so he threw out the drink he'd purchased and drove toward downtown. Olivia would get him back on track, thoughts of their growing connection made him feel guilty for thinking about Vi.

Using his shift as an excuse was a spur of the moment decision. He really needed to sort out his feelings. He almost apologized at the look Cassie gave him, but he just couldn't spend that much time close to Vi.

When he'd looked down into that ridiculously small car of hers and saw her looking up at him, his first instinct had been to kiss her senseless. Thankfully, he'd been able to resist the impulse—he was seeing Olivia and it wouldn't have been fair to her.

His phone rang, Olivia's ringtone pulling him from his musing. He hadn't even started the car yet, so he answered.

"Hey, beautiful," Dane crooned into the phone.

"Hi, Dane." He could hear the smile in her voice, prompting his lips to curl up.

He ran his fingers through his hair. "What's up?"

"I'm sure by now you've heard that Violet is home, and there's a party at The Pub tonight."

"Yeah, I heard, but I'm on shift until ten. Cassie isn't too happy with me about it, but them's the breaks in law enforcement."

"I already called and talked to Sam for you. He'll be in to take over your shift at five, so you'll have time to shower and change before you pick me up. I'll be waiting…and you're welcome." He heard her giggle as she hung up.

Olivia had a knack for getting her own way, but what was he to do? She was his boss's daughter. Some days he wondered if he was doing the right thing. Besides being the sheriff's daughter, her family was intertwined with the Millers. He sighed, started his cruiser, and pulled out of the parking lot to finish what was left of his shift.

Violet unlocked the door and stepped into the house, bracing herself for the inevitable tackle from an excited dog. The only question was which dog would get to her first. Duke, their current English Mastiff, ran up and leaned against her legs, almost knocking her over. He was followed by the two rescues, Molly, a bully mix, and Nelson, a lab/shepherd mix. Molly turned in circles while Nelson excitedly jumped up and down. Belly rubs and kisses took twenty minutes, and then she noticed a new rescue watching her from a dog crate.

"Oooh, what a sweetie," she cooed as she squatted next to the crate, the back of her hand held out for a sniff. One blue and one brown eye watched her as she opened the crate and reached in for a pet. The pup was some kind of husky mix, with distinctive husky markings but with a short coat. "You must be Rufus," she said as she picked up the puppy. "Welcome to the zoo."

She let the puppy roam for a while and then shooed them all out the back door to do their business, being sure to praise the puppy when he watered the tree.

"Come on guys, I gotta get unpacked." They all trotted in and waited patiently by the cupboard that held the dog cookies. After everyone had their snack, she put the puppy back in the crate and headed upstairs to unpack her bags. The rest of the stuff she'd collected over the last four years, including her furniture, would arrive the next day.

Violet sank down into the lavender scented bubbles, her mind going about a hundred miles an hour. Her secret was about to be exposed. Her fiancé—the one she had yet to tell anyone about—would be arriving just in time for the party that night. Her father was going to go ballistic because he hadn't even met him. Caleb was out of town when she graduated, and that would be the first strike against him. The second was that they'd only met six months ago. Strike three, though? He was a musician who made most of his money busking. She really hoped to have some time to talk to her parents about him before they announced their engagement.

After twenty minutes, she heaved herself out of the tub, disappointed that her bath hadn't been relaxing at all.

She rifled through her closet, looking for something special to wear. If she was going to have to announce her engagement, she needed to look her best. She pulled out her favorite dress. Long and flowy, it fit her hippie vibe to a T. With her red hair and fair skin, the green looked fabulous, making her eyes pop.

She was putting on her trademark dangly earrings when she heard her parents arrive home.

"Violet, honey?"

"Upstairs, Mom."

Cassie poked her head in the door. "Good, you're almost ready. I'm going to change while your dad is in the shower. We'll be ready to roll in about fifteen."

"Okay," she replied. She'd planned to drive herself until Caleb dropped the bombshell that he was there in Fairfield Corners.

A spritz of perfume and she was ready. To kill some time, she unpacked her other suitcase and moved the clothes into her dresser. *Now that Caleb's here, we'll need to find our own place.* Maybe the apartment above the bookstore was available, she'd have to ask her mom about it. At least she'd have furniture to fill it.

Her dad? Now that was going to be a difficult conversation. Moving in with Caleb before they were married wouldn't sit well with him.

Memories assaulted her when she stepped into The Pub behind her parents. She'd spent many a Saturday chasing her cousins around the tables. Now they were all grown up and beginning lives of their own. Somehow it was different now. While she was in college, she'd still felt like a kid. Now she considered herself an adult, something her dad would have to deal with.

Hugs were the order of the day, and they eventually all took their seats around tables that had been pushed together to accommodate their growing numbers. Mike the bartender distributed drinks and the party ensued, everyone chatting until they heard the door open.

Dane stood in the doorway, his arm over Olivia's shoulders, looking around as if surveying the mood of the room. He sauntered over to the group and pulled out a chair for his date directly across from Vi.

As they were shuffling seats, the door opened again.

"Caleb!" Violet cried as she stood, her chair scooting back with a screech across the floor, bringing everyone's attention to her.

She hurried over and took his hand. "Everyone, this is Caleb, my..." she stopped momentarily to build up her courage and then blurted, "fiancé."

"Oh my God. Why didn't you tell me?" her mother yelled as she hurried around the table. "When did this happen?"

Her father stared at her, his eyes narrowed. "Yeah, when exactly *did* this happen?" he ground out between gritted teeth. "And why didn't we meet him at your graduation?"

"Dad, really?" she snapped at him. "You didn't meet him because he was out of town that week for a job. He's a sound tech and a musician."

She pulled Caleb toward the table. "Caleb, this is my mom and dad, Cassie and Logan. Please ignore my dad's scowl, he seems to forget I'm an adult."

Cassie hugged him, "It's so nice to meet you, Caleb." She directed everyone to clear a space for another chair next to Vi's. "So, how did you two meet?"

Caleb took a sip of beer, probably to fortify himself for the grilling to come. "I was running the sound board for a local bar's open mic night. When Violet stepped out on stage and started singing, I was spellbound. Such a beautiful voice. Later that night, she walked right past me, and I didn't even recognize her as the angel who'd been singing, since I hadn't even noticed what she looked like." He gulped some more beer. "We started talking about music, and it was suddenly closing time."

Violet jumped into the conversation, "We've been dating for five months. I know it's fast, but we're sure about how we feel." She looked over at her dad, not surprised to see his scowl. What a hypocrite, he'd declared his love for Cassie after a short time, so why was it okay for him but not her?

"So, this music tech thing, it pays well?"

"Logan! Now is not the time…" Cassie started only to be shushed by her husband.

"It's the perfect time, seeing's how she kept him a secret. I want to know why."

"Dad, seriously? Can we talk about this later? Alone?"

He stood and stomped to the door, turning back to look at his errant daughter. "Tomorrow, Vivi, we *will* discuss this."

Too busy watching her father's antics, she failed to notice the look Dane shot Caleb, as if he wanted to take him out back and beat the shit out of him. He rubbed his temples.

Olivia put her hand on his arm. "You okay, Dane?"

"Just a headache. Do you think you could grab a ride home with your dad?" He looked across the table to where James and Marie were talking with Adam and Ragan.

"Are you sure you don't want me to go with you?"

"No, I just need some Tylenol and a few hours' sleep." He kissed her cheek. "I'll call you in the morning and we can meet for breakfast."

"Okay, that sounds nice." She stood and held her hand out to him. "I'll walk you out."

Violet watched as Dane left, his arm once again around Olivia's shoulders. *Wow, he didn't even say hi or 'nice to have you home'.* She turned when Caleb took her hand.

"You okay, Baby?"

"Yeah, just tired. It was a long drive today. How about I take you home?"

"Where are you staying? I can't have you at the house, not with the mood Dad's in." She looked up at him. "Let me call the bed and breakfast, it's about five minutes from here."

"I don't know if I can afford…"

"Don't worry about it, we'll get it taken care of. I know the lady who owns it, so she'll give us a break."

"Are you sure? I saw some cheap hotels in Fort Wayne."

"No reason for you to be driving that far every day." She pulled her phone out of her purse and dialed Mrs. DeHaven's number. "Besides, I'm hoping I'll have an apartment for us by next week."

Chapter Four

VIOLET

Violet twirled and giggled. Her dad had pitched a fit about Caleb moving in, but she had stood up to him. "I'm twenty-one and it's my decision. Besides, it's a bit hypocritical for you to be against Caleb moving in. You and Mom lived together before you got married."

He'd frowned at her, his arms folded across his chest.

"That's what I thought," she taunted. Knowing better than to push it any further she stood on tiptoe and kissed his cheek. "I love you, Daddy."

He relaxed slightly, his arms going around her in a hug. "Love you too, precious girl. I don't like it, but I'll keep my mouth shut."

"Thank you." She pulled her phone out of her pocket and started scrolling through her contacts. "Now, I need to ask Mom about the apartment above the store."

"Vivi, wait. Don't do that."

"Why not?"

"That's Dane's place now."

"Oh." She tapped her lips. "What about Uncle Adam's house over on Elm? Anybody living in it right now?"

"No, we've been doing regular drive-bys to keep an eye on it. Call him."

"A whole house to ourselves? That would be awesome. I hope we can afford the rent."

Logan grimaced.

"Sorry, I'm just excited."

He checked his watch. "I've got to get going. James is expecting me at the station in a few minutes. Keep us in the loop, would ya?"

"Sure, Daddy." Her attention returned to her phone. "Love you," she murmured as he walked out the door.

With a frown she turned off her phone. "Damn, he's not picking up." She ran upstairs to grab her purse, pausing to check her reflection in the full-length mirror.

~

She walked into The Pub and scanned the room, looking for Adam. "Hey Mike," she called when the bartender walked out from the store-room with a box in his hands, "is my uncle in his office?"

"Yeah. He's been putting out some fires with the Ground Zero tour, so I'm sure he'll be happy for the distraction."

"Thanks."

She practically skipped down the hallway, stopping in front of Adam's office door. It was ajar so she stuck her head into the room to see if he was still on the phone. "Uncle Adam?"

He looked up from the paperwork on his desk. "Violet, come in. You're a much prettier sight than these contracts." He stood and walked out from behind the desk and bent down to pull her into a hug. "I'm glad you're here." He stepped back and motioned for her to sit over on the couch. "You want a water or something else to drink?"

"No, I'm fine." She cleared her throat. "Dad said your rental house is empty. Caleb and I are looking for a place and I thought…"

Adam smiled. "Well, that's an easy answer. Yes, it's empty. What rent can you afford?"

"What do you normally get?"

"I usually get nine hundred a month. Is that good for you? If not, I'm sure we can come up with a number that makes it work."

"Nine hundred is fine. Between the two of us, that's totally doable. Oh, and what about pets?"

He grinned. He knew the new rescue would be hard for Violet to resist. "You fell in love with Rufus, didn't you?"

"Well, yeah. I've missed the chaos of having a dog or two around. I figured I better just start with one. That is, if it's okay with you. You are the landlord and all."

Adam laughed. "Like you need to ask. I never could say no to you and I'm not going to start now."

Adam sat next to her. "Listen, I had something I wanted to ask you. I saw videos of the concert you played in Philly this summer. You are really good."

She blushed. Adam's high opinion of her performance was a good sign, given his rockstar status and owning Sky's The Limit Records. "I know I still need to work on my…"

"Nonsense," he interrupted her. "You have stage presence, and that's not something easy to learn." He went to the desk and picked up a small stack of papers. "This contract is for the house band. I want you to sing here weeknights and any weekends that are not filled by other acts." He handed her the papers. "Is that something you'd be interested in?"

"What? I wasn't expecting this." She scanned the top sheet of paper. "Can I think about it?"

"Of course. Have someone look over the contract if you want."

"The house band makes this much a week?" she stared at the number there in black and white.

Adam laughed. "Yes, that's my standard rate."

"Oh wow," she breathed.

"Plus, when you're ready, I want to sign you on to Sky's The Limit. I think you've got the talent to make it big, if that's what you want."

"Oh my God, yes!" she yelled and jumped up. "I can't wait to tell Caleb! He'll be so excited."

"Go, have someone look over the contract and we'll meet again tomorrow at noon. We can sign the contract over lunch."

She picked up her purse. "Thank you so much."

He rummaged in the middle desk drawer and then tossed her a set of keys. "Don't forget these."

"What about the lease?"

"We'll sign that tomorrow, too, but this way you can move in today."

She wrapped him in a hug. "You're the best."

Adam snickered. "I have the feeling your dad's not going to think so."

She grinned. "True, but he'll just have to get over it." Digging in her purse for her phone, she hurried out the door.

Windows down, the breeze cooling off the hot interior of her car, she dialed Caleb, excited to tell him about the house.

Chapter Five

DANE

The door of The Pub swished closed behind him, shutting out the sun and heat of the August afternoon. He stood there, letting his eyes adjust to the lower light inside the building. Scanning the room, he zeroed in on an open table, winding his way around occupied chairs while nodding and greeting the people he knew. He took a chair and opened the menu, looking up when he heard her voice.

"Oh geez, it's crowded in here today. Looks like we'll have to wait for a table." She looked at her companion, Adam's daughter Jenna.

The sight of her hit him right in the solar plexus, and he exhaled a long breath as his heart thundered in his chest. Without thinking he waved and caught Jenna's attention.

"Oh hey, there's Dane. Looks like he's alone; we could share his table."

Vi gulped. This would be the first time she'd been face to face with him since the day he stopped her out on the highway.

"We shouldn't. Maybe he's waiting for someone."

"Oh, come on. He waved us over." Jenna watched as Vi stood frozen in place. "Seriously? He was your best friend. You're going to have to talk to him sometime." Jenna tapped her foot and glared at her.

Violet rolled her eyes and sighed, "Oh, all right."

"Good." She grabbed Vi's hand and dragged her toward Dane and the empty chairs around his table. "Hi, Dane. Thanks for this. I think the whole town decided to eat at The Pub for lunch today."

"No problem. What man wouldn't want two of the prettiest girls in town enjoying lunch with him.

"You better not let Olivia hear you say that," Jenna said with a smirk.

Vi sat across from Dane, her hands clasped together under the table. *Why does he want me to have lunch with him?*

Mike walked up, an order pad in his hand.

"You guys know what you want? It might be a few minutes, 'cause the waitress is late and it's just me."

Jenna piped up, "Just a cheeseburger and fries with a chocolate shake."

"Same for me," Vi nodded.

"Dane?"

"Make it three, but make my shake strawberry."

"Will do. I'll have this out to you as soon as I can." He looked over when the door slammed. "Oh, thank God. Our waitress finally showed."

Once the food arrived, Dane and Jenna chatted about the upcoming Harvest Dance.

"I'm sure Olivia is looking forward to it," Dane said as he pushed his empty plate off to the side. "She's been helping her mom plan the decorations for weeks."

Jenna's phone beeped with a text notification. "I'm sorry but I've got to run. Joey has a temp, so I've got to go pick him up. I'll see you two later."

Vi watched Jenna hurry out of The Pub, wishing she'd gotten up and gone with her. She turned back to the table and Dane changed seats so he was closer to her.

"I want to apologize for the way I acted on the highway last week. Seeing you in that ridiculous little car was a shock."

"Why? I'm sure Mom told you I would be home that day."

"Yeah, at home or here at the welcome party after I'd had a chance to psych myself up for it."

"Why would you have to psych yourself up? You're the one who left without so much as a 'see ya later'." She stood, her chair screeching as it moved across the floor. "I was devastated."

"Vi, I, …" he stumbled over the words, trying to get them from his brain to his tongue.

"What? You're sorry?" Her voice rose, "Well, fuck that." She whirled and stomped her way out the door.

"Jesus, what the hell was that about?" he asked himself.

The waitress walked over and placed the check on the table, watching him as she backed away.

"And she stuck me with the check. Great," he muttered as he reached for his wallet.

Chapter Six

One Month Later

VIOLET

Violet sat at the kitchen table and stared at the bank statement on her phone. There were the deposits for Caleb's paychecks and then, immediately after, withdrawals of almost the total of the deposit. They were both supposed to deposit enough money into the account to cover their bills. But this week, there was no deposit at all.

Rufus sat next to her chair and whined, as if sensing her mood.

She dropped her hand and scratched behind his ears. "At least I know you won't run out on the rent little guy. I think me and your daddy need to have a chat about our finances."

Luckily, her singing job at The Pub paid fairly well, plus there was the money she made working at the bookstore a couple days a week. There was also the money she was saving in a separate account to buy a new guitar. So, if she moved funds around, she'd have the money to cover the bills; but that wasn't the point.

It was getting late, and Caleb still wasn't home. He was coming home each day later and later, oftentimes she could smell the cheap booze he'd been drinking. She'd let it slide as she knew he was disap-

pointed he couldn't find a better paying job than as a gas station atten-
dant. No one needed an over-educated sound tech with an attitude
problem.

She stood at the stove stirring the bubbling sauce. Caleb loved her
homemade pasta sauce, and she wanted him to be in a good mood
before she asked him about the withdrawals and the missed deposit.
The door opened and closed, and then she heard his keys hit the dish
on the table behind the couch.

"Wow, something smells good. What's the occasion? Caleb asked
as he walked into the kitchen and went to the fridge for a beer. That
was another thing she wanted to talk to him about, the amount of beer
he was drinking each day concerned her.

"Nothing, just felt like pasta. You hungry?"

"Always. Let me know when it's done." He walked out of the
kitchen.

She heard the television turn on and him flopping onto the couch,
and that worried her, too. There was a time when he would have
offered to help her get dinner together, but now it was as if he'd
forgotten how. With a sigh, she returned to her sauce.

After throwing together a salad and popping some garlic bread in
the oven, she sat and sipped at a beer as she waited for the toast to be
done. *When did things change?*

She waited to broach the subject of the bank account until he'd
almost finished his spaghetti. "So, how was work today?" she asked.

"My boss hates me, and a customer complained that I was rude to
her."

"Oh, I'm sorry. Did you get a call back about that job at the radio
station?"

"No. What's with the third degree?"

"Well, I wanted to talk to you about our bank account." She sipped
at her beer and then continued, "I noticed quite a few withdrawals."

"What? Am I not allowed to spend the money I make working at
that shit job?" He stood and his chair screeched across the floor.
"Jesus."

"It's just…"

"Is there enough for the bills?"

"Well, yeah. The money I earn at The Pub is enough for now."

He slammed his beer on the table. "Rub it in my face that you're making more than me and doing what you love while I'm stuck in that shitty job in that shithole gas station." He stalked off, grabbing his keys on his way out the door.

She stared at the puddle of beer on the table, wondering how the conversation had deteriorated so quickly.

She woke to the smell of bacon. The pillow beside hers was undisturbed, no sign that Caleb had ever come to bed the night before.

Her feet hit the cold floor and she shivered. Time to invest in a pair of slippers now that fall weather was settling in. Rufus whined at her from his crate. "Daddy didn't let you out? Poor baby," she muttered as she opened the crate and gave the dog some scratches and pets.

Her feet freezing from the cold floor, she pulled on a pair of socks before ambling out to the kitchen to find Caleb standing at the stove turning bacon. Opening the back door to let the dog out into the fenced yard, she turned to watch Caleb at the stove while the dog did his business.

"Morning, sleepyhead," he said. "Look, I'm sorry about last night. I guess you making more money than I am struck a nerve." He took the carton of eggs out of the fridge. "I…"

"It's okay. I was just wondering about the withdrawals. You know I don't care how much money you make." Letting the dog back in, she frowned when he growled at Caleb. He just wasn't warming up to her fiancé at all.

Caleb transferred the bacon to a platter lined with paper towels and poured the eggs he'd scrambled into the pan. "I did something stupid a few months back and I owe money to some shady people. I've been trying to get the debt paid off, but…"

"You borrowed from a loan shark? What the hell for?"

Rufus whined at her raised voice.

"Jesus, can't you put that mutt in his crate or something?"

With a frown, she picked up the dog and took him back to his crate in the bedroom. "Sorry, Rufus, Daddy's in a bad mood this morning. I'll take you for a walk later, okay?"

She returned to the kitchen and poured herself some coffee before sitting at the table. "So, back to our conversation. Why did you need to borrow money? Especially from a loan shark."

"You know that guitar I bought you for your birthday?" He busied himself at the stove, stirring the eggs cooking in the skillet. "Well, I needed a car, and I couldn't afford that and the guitar, so I borrowed money from someone I thought was a friend."

"You shouldn't have done that. I didn't need that guitar."

"It was your birthday, and I knew you really wanted it."

"How much do you need?"

"No, I don't want…"

"Seriously, how much?" she poured herself more coffee. "I've got some money saved up."

He put his hands on the counter, his head hung low. "Five grand."

"What?" she coughed out as she choked on her coffee. "How much did you pay for that guitar?"

"Twenty-five hundred. I used the rest to buy my car. They're charging me so much interest I can't get ahead."

"I'll transfer it to your account." She picked up her phone and opened the banking app. "There. Pay them off." Her guitar account was now almost zero, but his safety was worth everything she had.

He scooped eggs from the pan onto a couple of plates. "I didn't want you to do that," he said with a sneer. "I can pay my own bills." He plopped the plates onto the table and turned back to the counter and spread butter on the toast that had popped up in the toaster.

"Tough. Now you owe it to me instead." She put the phone screen side down on the table. "A hundred a week until it's paid off."

He stomped out of the kitchen, leaving her to eat alone. She heard the front door slam. Something about his explanation didn't ring true.

When she'd checked out the guitar, it had been listed at a thousand, not twenty-five hundred."

She scraped the eggs into the trash, her stomach in knots from their argument. She should have taken a peek at his song so she'd know whether or not he was lying, but she'd promised herself she wouldn't do that to him. He wouldn't understand about her seeing music. Most people didn't, so she never bothered trying to explain.

She had a couple of hours until she needed to be at the bookstore, so she pulled clothes out of the hamper to throw a load into the washer. Checking pockets, she found a folded paper in his jeans. She almost put it on the dresser without looking at it, but their earlier conversation had her curious. She unfolded the paper and found it was actually a couple of papers. She opened the first to find an almost illegible note stating that he'd better start paying or they'd hurt *her*. With shaking hands, she folded the paper and laid it on the dresser. Unfolding the second, she found it was a betting slip. *What the hell is going on? Gambling, and a loan shark?* Good thing she'd given him the money to pay off his debt, but they were going to have a come to Jesus meeting when he got home. If he wasn't paying back the loan shark, the money was going somewhere. She checked the amount on the betting slip and choked. A thousand dollars...for one bet? Well, that explained where the money was going. Her stomach knotted as she dressed for her shift at the bookstore. *What has he gotten himself into?*

She'd been at the store for about an hour when Dane walked in. He sauntered over to her, and she couldn't help but notice how he moved as gracefully as a cat.

She rang up the customer who'd just walked up to the counter as Dane stood off to the side and waited. "Come again soon." She turned and glared at Dane. "What are you doing here?"

"I wanted to talk to you without your fiancé hanging around." He led her over to the seating area and motioned for her to sit next to him.

"I don't know if he told you, but I stopped him for speeding the other day. I ran his license; you know that's protocol."

"Oh God, now what?"

He frowned. "Are you having problems with him? Is he treating you right?"

She was surprised at his growly tone of voice. "Well, I did find out he owes money to a loan shark."

"What?" he barked, then stood and started pacing in front of the couch. "When I ran his license, it looked okay—until I noticed the age. The license is real, it's just not his. The license belongs to a fifty-nine-year-old man."

"I'm sure that has to be an error."

"After finding out he owes money to a loan shark, you're going to question my motives? I just don't trust the guy. Something about him…"

"You're just jealous! Butt out of my life, Dane. You gave up the right to do that when you left without a goodbye. I'll 'get along' with you for Mom and Dad but I don't have to actually like you. As a matter of fact, I think I hate you." She stood and stomped across the store to the office, slamming the door.

Dane

He stood and stared at the closed door, rubbing the muscles in the back of his neck. *Jesus, I'm just trying to look out for her.* He needed to get to the bottom of this before he took the info to Logan. He wanted to give the guy the benefit of the doubt—obviously Vi saw something in him that the rest of them didn't—but, God, the guy just seemed to radiate a slimy vibe. He trusted his gut instincts and his gut told him this guy was bad news.

He turned to leave the store and there he was, the slimy creep himself.

"Hi Dane, Violet here?"

His stomach churned. "Yeah, she's in the office." He watched as Caleb sauntered to the office, tapping the door before poking his head in. Something about him just wasn't right.

Caleb looked back at him before he stepped into the office, a sly grin on his face.

God, that guy made his gut go crazy. He stormed out of the store, intent on going back to the station to start digging into the creep.

Marching to his car, he wasn't watching where he was walking. He felt someone run into him, but he couldn't be bothered to stop. He waved and continued on until he heard his name.

"Dane."

He looked up and grimaced. Olivia. Damn, he was supposed to meet her for lunch. "Oh, hey Olivia. Sorry about that, I've got something on my mind."

Reaching up she cupped his cheek, "That's okay. What's got you so wound up?"

"That creep Violet is engaged to. Something about him…"

"Is it him, or would it be any guy that's engaged to her?"

"What? No, it's not like that."

"Stop, you're practically her big brother. You're allowed to be worried for her."

"I'm glad you understand because I sure don't," he said with a grin. He glanced at his watch. "It's a little early but you ready for lunch? I've got time right now."

She took his arm in hers and turned him back toward the bookstore. "Yes, but first I want to pick up the book I ordered last week."

He wanted to be anywhere but back in that store with that slimy creep. "Okay." He took her hand and kissed the back of it as they started back to the door.

He let her go when they entered the store. She went to the counter, and he wandered toward Caleb. Once he was sure Vi was occupied with Olivia, he stepped closer to Caleb.

"You hurt her and you'll answer to me." He put his hand on Caleb's shoulder and squeezed, hard. "Got it?"

Caleb grinned at him. "Oh yeah, I got it." He turned his head and looked at Violet. "I think you're the one who needs to take a step back. She's mine now. Oh, I know all about the broken little boy you used to be. And now you're hoping to play big brother to my fiancé again." He stepped closer and looked Dane in the eye, "She doesn't want anything to do with you. If you don't back off, I'll convince her to move as far away from this backwards little town as we can get." He stepped back and smiled. "Be the bigger man, Dane."

His radio squawked, "Dane, you available?" He waved at Olivia and pointed to his radio as he strode out the door. "Yeah, what you got?"

"10-50 PD out on Highway 30 near the north county line, fire has been dispatched."

"On my way." He tapped out a quick text to Olivia and hurried to his cruiser. Duty called, so the creep would have to wait.

Chapter Seven

DANE

Dane sped toward Vi and Caleb's, the background report on Caleb on the seat next to him in a folder. It had taken some time, but he'd found out Caleb's real last name a couple of days ago. And what he'd discovered made him want to hit something. No, not something—someone. No way was he letting his Vi marry a guy with a felony rape accusation on his record. He'd called the Dallas police department and had them send over the file. Reading the girl's statement made his stomach churn. If not for the broken chain of custody on the DNA evidence, he'd be in prison. Asshole got off on a stupid technicality.

Vi's car sat in the drive next to the house. He was relieved she was home because he didn't want to chase her all around the county with this news.

He saw the blinds twitch as he walked up the front sidewalk so he wasn't surprised when the door opened before he could knock.

"What do you want, Dane?"

"We need to talk about your fiancé." It was all he could do not to blurt out what he knew. The front porch was not where he wanted to do this.

"What about Caleb?" She frowned as she twisted her engagement ring around on her finger.

"Is he here?" He relaxed slightly when she shook her head no. At least they could talk about this alone. He was sure Caleb had all kinds of excuses for what had happened.

She stood in the doorway, frowning at him. "I know you don't like him, but seriously, you need to back off."

"Can we go in and talk? You really don't want to do this out here."

She led him to the living room and motioned to a chair. Rufus trotted over for some pets from Dane. "Wow, you're growing fast, big guy," he said as he stroked the dog's head.

He sat and laid the folder on the coffee table. "I'm sorry." He flipped open the file folder and moved it so she could read the papers inside.

"What is this?" she asked as she scanned the background report. "Felony? No way, this can't be right. This can't be my Caleb."

He pulled out the mug shot and showed it to her. "It's him." He rubbed the knot in the back of his neck as he looked at his shoes. "Keep going. There's a copy of the complaint and the charges filed." He continued to rub the back of his neck, wishing he was off duty so he could have a drink. "I'm worried about you."

She looked up at him, her face pale. "Is this real? It's not something you made up to get me away from him?"

"I wish it wasn't. According to the arresting officer, Caleb laughed about it during the trial." He ran his hand through his hair. "And his real name is Caleb Stratham. For some reason, he lied about his identity."

Vi jumped up, gagging, and fled the room. He got a washcloth out of the linen closet and wet it under the tap, filling a glass on the counter with cool water. Retching sounds from the bathroom made him frown. *How could she have fallen for Caleb's bullshit?* He stood in the bathroom doorway, his back to her, and waited until she was finished.

After Vi took a shaky breath and sat back on her heels, he handed her the water and watched as she swished and spit before kneeling next to her and wiping her face with the cloth. Rufus watched from the doorway, whining.

"How could he…" she started before burying her face in his shirt.

He wrapped his arms around her and pulled her closer, his heart aching at her sobs. God, why had he made that promise to Logan? His feelings for her hadn't waned in the seven years they'd been apart, damned things've been in hiding until rushing back to the surface the first time he saw her again.

Slowly, he lowered himself until he was sitting on the floor and pulled Vi onto his lap. He kissed the top of her head and hummed, knowing that had always calmed her in the past. Her sobs tore into his heart. That asshat didn't deserve her—he deserved to be sitting in a jail cell.

As her sobs tapered off, he reached around her and grabbed a roll of toilet paper from under the sink.

"I should have known something wasn't right with him. Rufus growls at him constantly." She hiccupped and wiped at the tears on her face. "How did I not see it?"

"Here," he said as he handed her the roll. "You want some tea? It will help settle your stomach."

"How can you still care about me after what happened?" Her tear-stained face looked up at him from her spot on the floor.

"What are you talking about?"

"It was my fault you got sent away. You should hate me." She sniffed and blew her nose, shaking her head sadly. "All my fault," she murmured.

"Where in the hell did you get that idea? It wasn't your fault."

"I let you take me out to The Island. I knew Dad would be furious if he found out, and he was. He sent you away and it was all my fault. I should have said no."

"You didn't get the letter I left for you? I was up all night writing it."

"The only letter I got was the one you mailed after boot camp." She stood and splashed some water on her face before turning to face him. "By that time, I thought you hated me so I never opened it. I didn't want to know. I told myself that if I didn't open it, I could pretend you didn't hate me."

"I could never hate you, silly girl." He hugged her again. "Let's go make you some tea and talk about this."

"But where is it?"

"Where is what? The letter?" At her nod he answered, "Where would I have left an important letter for you?"

"Oh my God! It's behind the loose brick, isn't it? God, I was so stupid. I should have checked…" She stepped back and looked up into his face. "I need to read it. Right now. Let's go," she said as she grabbed his hand and pulled him toward the front door.

Just then his radio crackled, the dispatcher's voice notified him of an attempted robbery at the gas station just outside of town. "I've got to go. You okay to drive over to your mom and dad's?"

"Yeah."

He kissed her forehead, "I want you to stay there."

"Why?"

"I don't want you in this house alone with Caleb."

"I can handle him." She stared at him as if daring him to contradict her.

"I know you think you can, but I'm afraid he might get violent. So please, talk to him with other people around; preferably me or your dad." He ran his hands through his hair. "I gotta leave. Promise me, Vi."

"Okay," she replied. "Go. Do your job. Keep the town safe."

Dane hurried to his cruiser and climbed in, hitting the sirens and lights before pulling away with a screech of tires.

Violet

Violet unlocked the door and let herself into her parent's house, Rufus at her heels on his leash. Duke, Molly, and Nelson trotted around her, tails wagging and noses nudging her hands asking for pets. "Okay guys, that's enough." As much as she wanted to check the loose brick first thing, she followed the dogs to the kitchen and gave them treats while praising them. Once they settled, she grabbed a bottle of water from the fridge and walked into the living room, berating herself for not checking their hiding spot sometime over the last seven years.

She ran her hand along the front of the mantle, looking at the family photos on display. Now that she was there, she was afraid to check their spot. What if it was empty? Surely, he wouldn't have lied about it.

She knelt in front of the fireplace and wiggled the loose brick out of its place, sticking her hand into the hole. At first, she felt nothing—and then, the edge of an envelope. Trembling fingers grasped the paper and pulled it out slowly. She gasped when her name became visible through the dust on the front, written in the sloppy handwriting of an eighteen-year-old boy. Handwriting so familiar she could almost have copied it exactly.

Blowing the dust off it into the fireplace, she turned it over and carefully pried the flap open, not wanting to take the chance of ripping the brittle paper.

My Vi,

I've tried over the last two weeks to tell you this, but I couldn't do it. I couldn't stand to see sadness in your eyes or on your face. But now I have to, and it's killing me inside.

I'm leaving. I made a promise to your dad and I don't want to go, but I have to. I haven't even left yet and my chest feels like there's a huge hole where my heart should be.

When I decided to join the Army, I knew it would hurt you. Please understand that I need to do this for me, even though it breaks my heart to leave you.

I'll miss you so much, so please write to me. I'll know you've forgiven me for being a spineless idiot when I get your first letter.

Love you always and forever,

Your Dane

A tear dropped onto the paper. *How did I not know?* She should have thought to check their spot. All this time she'd blamed herself for his leaving.

She sat on the hearth and held the letter to her chest. Letting the tears flow down her cheeks, she was careful to keep them away from the fragile paper. She didn't hear her mother unlock the door or her greetings to the dogs.

"Violet, honey, you okay?"

"What?" She looked up at her mother.

"Are you okay? You've been crying." Cassie sat next to her daughter. "Is this about Caleb? The information Dane found about him?"

"Actually, no. I completely forgot about that." She wiped the tears off her cheeks with one hand, the other holding tight to the letter, not even wanting to let go of it long enough for her mom to read it. She forced herself to hold it out to her, "I finally found this."

"Oh, wow. You can practically feel the love emanating from the words written on the page," she said when she finished reading it.

"I thought it was my fault he left, that Dad had sent him away because he took me out to The Island that night."

"Oh sweetie," Cassie said as she pulled her daughter in for a hug. "I thought Dane told you. We thought you were mad at him for leaving."

"No, it was guilt." She stood and brushed at the seat of her jeans. "I could use a cup of tea, and some bourbon in it wouldn't be refused."

They walked to the kitchen. "Mom, there's just one thing I don't understand. What promise did he make to Dad?"

"I don't know," Cassie replied as she filled the teakettle with water and set it on the stove.

The dogs took off for the front door barking when the doorbell rang.

"I'll get it, Mom," Vi called out as she walked out of the kitchen. She looked through the peephole and frowned. Caleb. She wasn't ready to deal with him yet, but she guessed she didn't have a choice. She put on the chain and opened the door a crack as Rufus growled menacingly.

"Violet, sweets, open the door. It's me." He stood on the porch, his hair ruffling in the breeze.

"I don't want to talk to you, Caleb."

"What's going on?" he asked, frowning. He turned around when Dane answered for her.

41

"She knows what you did, you worthless piece of shit."

Caleb stood tall but was still almost three inches shorter than Dane. "Oh, for God's sake. That was a bunch of lies. Bitch set me up. She wanted it."

With a growl, Dane balled his fist and ground out, "No one asks for what you did to that girl. The girl you supposedly loved."

"Lies. It's all lies."

"I'm following you over to Violet's house so you can pack up your shit and get out of town." He stood and crossed his arms over his chest, the badge on his shirt pocket flashing in the sun. When Caleb didn't move Dane growled, "Now."

Caleb turned back to Violet, his face set in fury. "Violet, call off your pet policeman."

"You better do what he says. You aren't wanted here." She took off her engagement ring and threw it at him. "Get out of my house...*NOW.*"

"Well then, you owe me the money I deposited..."

"Nope. Don't even try it. I know you've been withdrawing everything you deposited and then some, plus there's the five grand I gave you. Just get out of my house."

The red crept up Caleb's face.

"You heard her. Leave, now, or I'll arrest you for trespassing." Dane stepped around Caleb and handed Vi a key. "Adam had the locks changed."

Caleb glowered. "And why would he do that?"

"Because I explained the situation. Deal with it." He turned and watched Caleb saunter down the sidewalk to his car. "I've got to go and make sure he gets his stuff out of your house."

"We're not done talking about this."

He ran his hands through his hair and sighed. "I know." Keying his radio, he notified the dispatcher he would be on a call as he hurried to his cruiser to follow Caleb to Vi's house.

They'd no sooner returned to the living room when Logan stomped into the house. He grabbed Vi and pulled her in for a hug. "Are you okay?" he asked as he stepped back to look into her eyes.

"Yeah, Daddy. I'm fine." She wiped an errant tear away. "I'm not fine with Dane running a background check on my former fiancé without asking me. Who does he think he is?"

"Someone who cares about you. And what's this I hear about you giving that asshole five grand?"

Ignoring his comment about the money, she glared at him. "I have a bone to pick with you, too." She folded her arms across her chest, mimicking her father's go-to stance when he wasn't pleased about something. "Why did you let me think you sent Dane away because we got caught after curfew out at The Island?"

He pulled her over to the couch and motioned for her to sit, taking a seat next to her. "What are you talking about? Didn't he tell you he was leaving?" He rubbed the stubble on his chin. "You really didn't know?" Shaking his head, he whispered to himself, "Dane, you're a dumbass."

Violet giggled. "I heard that, and I agree. Did you know he called Adam and had him change the locks? Like that wouldn't be the first thing I did after I found out the truth about Caleb."

"We men tend to forget how resourceful our women are. You know he still cares about you, right?"

"Oh, I don't know…I think I'm back to being the annoying little sister." She led her father back to the kitchen, fixed a cup of tea, and handed it to him.

"You sure about that? I don't think you've ever been an annoyance to Dane." He sipped at the hot beverage with a sigh. She knew how much her father liked his tea.

"Yeah, I'm sure. He needs to understand I'm not that little girl anymore." She stirred her cup of tea and then blew over the top to cool it before taking a sip. "I'm all grown up and can take care of myself."

Chapter Eight

VIOLET

Violet stepped around a couple locked in an embrace in the dark hallway that led from backstage to the bar. "Oops, excuse me," she mumbled as she stepped past them into the main bar area.

She was ready for a beer. Adam had told her she could skip tonight. She could see in his eyes that he was worried about her and her break up with Caleb. Any girl would be upset if she found out the guy she thought she loved and was going to marry was a rapist. Why were men such twats?

She was grateful that Dane found that out before she'd married the creep, but she was still mad that he'd looked into her ex behind her back. She didn't need him looking out for her. Seriously, between him and her dad, you could practically cut the testosterone with a knife.

She hitched herself up onto a barstool and Pete, the new bartender, slid a coaster in front of her before setting a glass of ice water on it. "Thanks. I'll take a beer, too. Is Adam still here?"

"I think he's in the office. I can call and check?"

"Nah, I'll catch him whenever."

The cool water soothed the slight scratchiness of her throat. The weather was changing and her allergies were kicking in. A hot tea with lemon would be her first order of business when she got home to her now empty house. At least she didn't have to worry about Caleb still having a key. Good riddance. How could he think she wouldn't find out he'd raped his previous fiancée or that Baker wasn't even his real last name?

She drained her beer and looked over at Pete, leaving him a couple of bills for a tip.

"You leaving?"

"Yeah," she stifled a yawn. "It's late and I'm beat." '

"Let me call security. You don't need to be walking out back alone."

"Oh geez. You people think he's going to attack me or something?" she muttered. "Don't bother, I'm parked right near the door, directly under the light."

"Your uncle will fire me if I let you go out there alone."

"Okay. Have them meet me by the back door in five minutes."

She hurried down the hall and picked up her guitar case and coat. Leaning next to the outer door, she stifled another yawn.

She grinned when Colt LeBrea walked up. He'd been working security for her uncle since Adam made it big. "I didn't know you were back. The Ground Zero guys must have made it home in one piece."

"Yes, they did. Look at you, all grown up. You sounded really good up there tonight." He opened the door and stepped out in front of her, holding her back with a hand on her arm. "You know the drill. Let me take a look."

He scanned the parking lot and let her walk beside him to her car. "This is yours? It looks like a toy my son would play with."

"Not everyone wants to drive around in a tank," she laughed, referencing his preference for big-ass trucks.

"I think this would fit in the bed of my truck." He said with a laugh.

"I'll have to call you the next time I need a tow."

"Drive safe," he said, shutting her door after she climbed in.

Neither of them noticed Caleb's car parked in the back of the lot where the shadows made him easy to miss. He scowled as Violet drove away.

Violet parked in the drive. She hadn't noticed the car that followed her from The Pub. She walked into the house and locked the door behind her, looking out the front window when she heard a car drive by. *A cruiser. So either Dad or Dane is checking up on me.* Sigh.

Rufus barked when she didn't immediately come to let him out of his crate.

"Oh baby, I'm coming." She opened the crate and he jumped up, giving her doggy kisses.

"Come on, Rufus. Outside first, then we can cuddle. She let him out the back door, thankful Adam had fenced in the back yard. Rufus trotted around, sniffing and exploring until she told him it was time to potty, which he did; such a smart puppy.

Once he was done and back in the kitchen, she gave him a treat and some praise. How could she have ignored how Rufus had hated Caleb? That should have been her first clue that he wasn't who she thought. Now, the dog absolutely loved Dane. "You and me both, buddy," she mumbled as she pulled a bag of chips out of the cupboard and grabbed a soda from the fridge. It was Thursday night, and she needed a junk food binge.

Remote in hand, she climbed onto the couch and pulled the blanket over herself, patting the cushion next to her for Rufus to join her. She pulled up her favorite series on her streaming service and settled in to watch.

Dane

He peeked in through the front window and saw Vi asleep on the couch, Rufus curled up beside her.

Feeling a bit like a peeping Tom, he let himself in with the extra key Adam had given him. He closed the door and turned to find the dog growling at him.

"Good boy, Rufus," he said. "We need to protect her, even when she doesn't want it."

Using the flickering light from the television to guide him, he picked her up, blanket and all, and carried her to the bedroom. Once he had her settled in the bed, he tucked the blankets around her the way he knew she liked.

He stared down at her in the dark, just listening to her breathe. "Don't worry Vi, I won't let anyone hurt you."

He bent over and kissed her forehead. He stilled when she stirred and mumbled, "Thanks Dane." On some level, she knew it was him. His heart thumped in time to her steady breaths, attuned to her in the way it had always been.

Rufus jumped up on the bed and circled three times before settling in against her legs.

Dane smiled. "Okay, you got this. Keep her safe, buddy."

He turned and walked out, checking all the doors and windows before he left, locking the door behind him. Now he could finish his shift knowing she'd made it home safe. At least that ass was away from her.

Violet

She snuggled into the warmth of her pillow. Her eyes popped open. How did she get here? Last she remembered she was watching television with Rufus. The dog felt her legs move and raised his head to look at her.

"How did I get here? And why aren't you in your crate? I hope I don't find any surprises."

She stumbled out to the kitchen to start the coffee, her feet shuffling along in her socks. *That's weird, I usually take off my socks before bed.* Hmmm… She found a note taped to the coffee maker.

Stopped by but you were asleep. Put you to bed.

Dane

Well, that explained that, but how did he get in? She was sure she'd locked the door. Her phone rang and she hurried back to the bedroom to get it off the charger.

Dane. Just the person she needed to yell at. "What the hell, Dane? Breaking into people's houses now, are you?"

He laughed. "Adam asked me to stop in and check on the…washer."

"After ten p.m.?"

"Well, I was driving by and thought it was as good a time as any. The television was on, so I stopped. I knocked but you didn't hear me. You didn't even hear Rufus growl at me when I let myself in with the key."

"You have a key? You need to give that to me."

"No, that's not going to happen. What if you need me to come and check on your washer?"

She could hear the smile in his voice and imagined how it would light up his whole face. She shook her head. *Sometimes he can be so goofy.* She had to remind herself that he was dating Olivia, so she had no claim on him now.

"Well, thanks for getting me to bed. Don't do it again." She hung up and returned to the kitchen, she needed caffeine before she tried to figure out what his grumpy ass was up to now.

Sufficiently caffeinated and dressed in jeans and running shoes, she clipped the leash on Rufus's collar and walked out the front door, careful to make sure it was locked.

Rufus stared across the street and growled, low and menacing.

"What's up Rufus? I don't see anything?"

His attention returned to her. He followed her down the sidewalk and around the corner.

A brisk twenty-minute walk and she was at her parents' place, climbing the steps to the big front porch. Her mom had decorated for fall with some corn stalks and a cute scarecrow sign that read 'Happy Fall'. She knew the pumpkins would come out soon as it was almost time for the Harvest Dance, the unofficial start of Fall in Fairfield Corners.

"Mom, you home?" she yelled as she closed the door behind her, wondering where the dogs had gotten off to. Seeing the leashes weren't in their place near the back door, she knew her mom must have taken them out for a walk.

She let Rufus off his leash and went to the kitchen to start some coffee since the fall breeze was chilly. The coffee pot gurgled as she climbed the stairs to the attic door. Her old record player was up there somewhere, and she'd bought a vinyl album to cheer herself up. She'd tried to play it on her turntable but discovered it was broken and needed to be fixed. *Add that to the list of stuff I need to take care of this week.* So, if she wanted to listen to the record now, she'd have to find her old portable player. She could grab the rest of her collection of albums while she was here, too, as she'd only taken a few with her to school.

She spied the sticker-covered case over in the far corner. *Why is it that every time I look for something up here it is always back in that creepy-assed corner?*

The floor creaking under her feet gave her the willies, so she hurried over, picked it up, and raced back to the door. Flipping off the light, she ran out the door and slammed it behind her. She didn't know why, but that corner of the attic always creeped her out big time.

After using a damp cloth to clean off the dust, she plugged in the record player and put on one of her albums, smiling when it worked. She did a little happy dance, turning when she heard the front door open. Rufus took off barking.

"Hello, Rufus. You came for a visit." She heard her mother say above the din of excited dogs. "Where's your momma?"

"In the kitchen Mom." She replied.

Cheeks pink from the cool breeze, her mother came in and hugged her. "Wasn't expecting to see you today. Oh good, you made coffee. That will warm me up." She pulled coffee mugs off the hooks under the cupboard and set them next to the pot. "What brings you by today?"

"What, I need a reason?"

"No, but you were just here yesterday…"

"I needed my old record player. I bought an album, but my turntable isn't working."

The coffeepot gurgled and gasped through the last of its brewing cycle. Cassie poured some into both mugs and added creamer.

"So, how is it living alone again?" her mother asked over the top of her coffee mug. At Violet's hesitation she continued, "Tell me the truth. Your dad isn't here looking all judgy."

"Well, ain't that the truth," she said with a laugh. "Seriously though, he was a slob; and if I had to pick up his dirty clothes from the floor right in front of the hamper one more time..."

Her mom sipped her coffee and snickered. "I'm lucky. Your dad is a bit of a neat freak so I've never had that issue."

"I guess I was just used to having my own space and doing things my way. It was supposed to be his home too." She poured herself some more coffee and turned around to lean against the counter.

"Well, now you don't have to worry about it." Another sip. "Give and take, that's the basis of a good marriage, aside from the whole love thing."

The dogs came tearing through the kitchen, barking like crazy. "Sounds like someone's here," Violet commented as she went toward the front door, curious.

Peeking out the curtains she spied Dane walking up the porch steps. Her hand went to her hair. *I probably look a hot mess. It's so windy today, I should have braided it.*

Her mom stood in the kitchen doorway and smiled, watching the inner war within her daughter play out across her face. They would figure it out on their own soon enough, they just needed to hurry up. She wanted grandbabies.

Violet grimaced. *Why am I worried? He's with Olivia, Dane is just a friend, now.* She stepped back when Dane walked in.

He looked at Cassie and asked, "Do you know where Vi is? I wanted to talk to her. Her car is at her place but she's not there."

Cassie pointed at Violet, whose cheeks were turning red.

"Oh, uh, hey," he said. "I...uh...just wanted to make sure you were doing okay after what happened."

She stared into her coffee, as if it held the answer. "I'm good."

Cassie interjected, "You have time for some coffee? Violet made a pot and there's plenty."

Dane followed her to the kitchen, and Violet brought up the rear with Rufus at her heel. Rufus sat and looked at her and then at the door.

"You need to go out?" Cassie asked. "Come on then," she said as she opened the door.

Violet caught Dane watching her. "What? I know my hair's a mess, the wind…"

"Just trying to decide if your answer was the truth. I mean, you thought you loved the guy and found out he'd been lying to you for months."

"Surprisingly, I'm good. I think deep down I knew he wasn't right for me; that something was off." She picked up a spoon and checked her reflection in the back of it.

"You look fine. Why do women obsess about how their hair looks?"

She threw the spoon at him, which he caught out of the air. *Cocky S.O.B.* she thought. "I just don't want to look like I was dragged backwards through that knothole in the tree out back."

She watched a corner of his mouth tip up into the smirk that made her knees weak. *Seriously Vi, get a grip. He's dating one of your best friends.* Mentally berating herself for thinking those kinds of thoughts about someone who was obviously taken, she picked up her mug and turned around to fill it with more coffee.

"You could never look…" he stopped as if he thought better of finishing that sentence. "Never mind." He gulped the rest of his coffee and set the mug in the sink. "Well, anyway, I was worried when you didn't answer the door but your car was there. I'm glad you're okay."

He turned and almost ran out of the house, saying something about needing to get back on patrol.

"What was that all about?" she whispered to herself.

"I saw Dane leave."

She nodded. "He said something about getting back to work. Did you think he was acting weirder than usual?"

Cassie smiled. "I think he's working through some stuff."

"I know we've talked about the whole him leaving thing and I thought we were okay, but…"

"Give him some time. You both ignored a lot of feelings for seven years. It may take a while to get back to where you were as friends."

Vi picked up her coat. "I should get home. I have a new song I'm working on, and I'd like to have it ready for my set tomorrow."

Cassie pulled her into a hug. "Let me drive you home. You should be more careful after what happened with Caleb."

"I suppose."

"Oh, and just to let you know—because I'm sure your dad didn't say anything to you—they'll be installing a security system at your house tomorrow."

"I'm not surprised. Actually, it will make me feel safer."

Twenty minutes later, she was sitting on her couch with her guitar and staring at the paper in front of her. The song, which had been flowing out of her the day before, was now gone.

"Well, shit." She aimlessly strummed the guitar, hoping the notes would reignite her inspiration. She started humming a new tune, the melody seeming to come out of her fingertips to the strings of the guitar.

"What I thought lost is found again." She thought for a moment, singing the lyric in her head. "That's not too bad," she mused as she wrote it down, noting the melody. "Let's see what we can do with this."

She strummed away, the musical inspiration flowing. Busy writing the lyrics, she didn't see the face just outside her window.

Chapter Nine

DANE

He watched Olivia walk toward him. *Why can't I love her?* She was beautiful, inside and out, but the feelings just weren't there. If he was being honest with himself, he knew why.

"Sorry I'm late. I was helping Mom with the plans for the Harvest Dance, and I wasn't watching the time. Have you been here long?"

"No, just five minutes or so." He smiled at Mike when he set a mug of his favorite beer in front of him. "Thanks, man." Throwing some bills on the tray to cover the beer and a drink for Olivia, he looked at her and asked, "Your usual?"

At her nod Mike headed back to the bar.

"You look tired. Long day?" she asked, taking his hand in hers.

God, he hated this part. "Yeah." He sipped at his beer, trying to come up with the words to break it off without hurting her. She was great. He was the one who couldn't commit to her. "I need to talk to you about something."

Mike set her drink in front of her and hurried off to another table.

"I wondered when this would happen." She rubbed her thumb over the back of his hand.

"What?"

"I think I knew when we first started dating that this was bound to happen. You're still in love with her, aren't you?" She squeezed his hand before letting go to take a sip of her drink.

"Who?"

"Violet, of course. Who else have you loved since you were what, seven?"

He gulped his beer; he had no idea it had been so obvious. "I... well, yeah."

With a smile, she reassured him, "It's okay. I knew she'd be back, someday."

"I'm sorry. I tried to move on but..."

"Even with you two arguing almost obsessively, everyone can see how you two feel about each other."

His attention shifted to the stage where his Vi had taken a seat on a stool and was adjusting the height of the mic. His attention was riveted on her as she strummed some chords and sang a song about loneliness and heartbreak. The lyrics ripped into his soul when he realized they were about him. About when he'd left, and she thought he was gone for good.

Olivia leaned over and spoke into his ear, "See? Totally in love. You're mesmerized by her."

"Huh?" he asked, looking at her.

"When she's around, your attention is focused on her alone."

He grinned at her sheepishly. "Can't help it. She's like a porch light and I'm a moth."

Violet

She was halfway through her last set when she watched Dane give her one last look before getting up and leaving. Something inside her deflated. She was hoping he'd stay so they could finally talk without anyone around.

She was packing up her guitar when there was a knock on the dressing room door . "Come in," she called out as she snapped the closures and reached for the guitar she'd borrowed from her uncle.

"Great show tonight, especially the acoustic set." Adam said as he walked into the room.

"Thanks for the loaner. I can't believe I forgot to bring my acoustic tonight."

"No problem. Listen, I'm here because there's someone in my office who would like to talk to you."

"Oh, okay. I was hoping to go find Dane so we could hash things out, but I can do that tomorrow."

Adam turned quickly so she wouldn't see his smile. "Gotta go. I promised Ragan I'd be home early tonight."

"Thanks again," she called to his retreating back.

She set her guitar case near the door, knowing it would be safe until she could retrieve it. It was a quick walk up the stairs to the office overlooking the bar. She knew her uncle enjoyed keeping an eye on things from up there.

The door to the office was ajar, so she knocked lightly and pushed it open. The lights were low and all she could see was the silhouette of a man.

"Ummm, hello? Adam said you wanted to talk…"

She gasped when he turned and saw his face. *Dane.* Now that they were face to face, her mind went blank.

She watched his face as his expression went from thoughtful to almost scared. "Is something wrong? Is it Dad? Or Mom?"

He stood and shoved his hands in his pockets. "No, nothing like that. I didn't mean to alarm you."

"What then? You look almost, scared."

"Well, I guess I am. Scared, I mean."

Now she was worried. He'd been in the Army, for goodness sake, so what did he have to be afraid of? She hurried over and took his hand in hers. "What's wrong?" She let herself peek at his song, but the low light of the office made it hard to make out.

"I broke things off with Olivia tonight." He pulled his hand out of hers and shoved it back in his pocket.

"Oh, I'm sorry. She didn't look upset when she left." She'd been singing that song she'd written when she was fourteen and Dane had just left. She hoped that wasn't the reason…

"Oh, she wasn't. She told me she'd been expecting it. Said she could see what I didn't want to admit to myself."

Vi watched Mike clearing tables and putting chairs up in preparation for the cleaning crew to do the floor. Arms folded over her chest to keep herself from reaching out to him again, she turned and looked back at him. He was staring at her as if she'd vanish into a puff of smoke any second. "What's going on, you're acting weird."

"I guess I need to explain some things." He ran his hands through his hair which now stood up in spikes, making him look like his younger self. "There's a reason I hardly spoke to you that day out on the highway." He sat on the couch and hung his head, rubbing at the muscles in the back of his neck. He looked up into Vi's eyes.

"I was an ass to you because the need to kiss you was so strong, I was afraid I was going to ravish you right there on the side of the highway. You sat there looking so calm after I hadn't seen you for seven years. Seven years without so much as a letter."

"I'm sorry about that. I…"

"Let me finish." He took a deep breath and continued. "Those feelings I wrote about that night before I left? I'd managed to keep them at bay, but one look at you and there they were again. You sat there in that ridiculous little car which perfectly fits your personality."

A tear threatened to escape and roll down her cheek. "Why did you wait until now to tell me this?"

"Because I made a promise to your dad. I promised I would let you grow up and live your life." He blew out a breath. "I understood at the time. You were only fourteen and hadn't even been on a real date. He was worried and I didn't blame him."

"But surely he didn't mean that we could never be together?"

He shrugged. "And then when you never wrote, I thought… Well hell, I don't know *what* I thought. I mean, now I know you never saw my letter but to not receive anything from you was the worst. I honestly thought you hated me."

"But…"

"Let me finish. Please."

She got up and paced the length of the room.

"And then to see you again without having any time to prepare myself to keep up the disinterested façade? The only thing I could do was get through it as quickly as possible and get away from you."

She dropped to her knees in front of him and took his hands in hers. "Thank you for explaining. I thought I'd done something to make you hate me."

"I could never hate you, Vi."

"Now it's my turn to explain some things." She kissed the back of his hands. "Not reading your letter wasn't the reason I didn't write. It was because I felt guilty."

"Guilty? Why? You didn't do anything?"

"Remember, I had no idea you'd been planning to leave. I was sure I was the reason you left, that Dad sent you away because we got caught out at The Island."

"That wasn't your idea, it was mine. Why would you think that?"

"Because I was fourteen, and the boy I loved with all of my soul left without a word. I was devastated." Her breath hitched and a sob rose from the depths of her being.

"Hey, don't cry." He pulled her up into his arms and then swung around so they were lying on the couch. "No matter what happened in the past, we both know the truth now." He kissed the top of her head and held her close.

Dane

"What the hell?"

Dane blinked and looked up into the face of a surprised Adam.

"Crap, we fell asleep. What time is it?"

"Eight a.m."

"Well, shit. I'm supposed to be on shift."

"Logan is going nuts trying to find you."

"I should have heard my phone. Crap. I forgot I silenced it last night while I was waiting up here for Vi and didn't want any distractions." He carefully pulled his phone out of his pocket, trying to not disturb Violet who was draped over him asleep. One glance at the phone and he grimaced. "Dead. Can I borrow your cell?"

Adam unlocked his phone and handed it to Dane.

Dialing Logan's number, he sighed as he waited for him to answer.

"Hey Logan, it's me. My phone is dead."

Dane held the phone away from his ear when Logan yelled, "Where are you? Have you seen Violet? She's missing, and I've been looking…"

"She's here, she's safe."

Vi opened her eyes and blinked at him sleepily.

"Hey beautiful. Your dad is looking for you." He handed the phone to her.

"Daddy?"

"Where are you? Your mother got worried when she got to your place this morning to pick you up to go shopping, and you weren't there."

"I'm at The Pub. I'm sorry, something came up and I…"

"How did Dane know to look for you there?"

"I, uh, we…" She sat up and squared her shoulders. "I was here with him all night."

"Oh. Well, as long as you're safe. Call your mother."

Violet handed the phone back to Dane who handed it to Adam.

Adam stuck the phone in his pocket. "I'll, uh, give you two some time." He walked out the door and pulled it shut behind him.

"Is your phone dead, too?" Dane asked with a smile.

"No clue. It's down in the dressing room with my guitar."

With a frown he growled, "You walked up here to meet someone without your phone on you? What if it was some creeper?"

"Uncle Adam wouldn't have left me alone with anyone dangerous. Now, I've got to get home. Poor Rufus probably thinks I abandoned him."

Chapter Ten

VIOLET

The next morning, Violet awoke to the sound of breaking glass and Rufus barking. She sat up on the couch and turned off the television, straining to hear any sound out of place. *Crap, I must have forgotten to set the alarm system again.*

The creak of a board in the hallway had her scrambling to find her phone as the dog stood in front of her and growled at the dark hallway. She mentally kicked herself when she remembered it was charging in the bedroom. "Shit," she muttered, looking for something she could use as a weapon. When the intruder strode into the living room, she gasped.

"Caleb? What are you doing here? What do you want?"

Caleb sneered at her, "I want you, and I want my book back."

His face was twisted into a scowl. How had she ever thought he was handsome? "I don't have anything of yours."

"I hid it. I couldn't grab it with that cop breathing down my neck. He'd have wondered why I'd hidden it. Couldn't have that."

She grabbed a heavy brass candlestick from the bookshelf and put the wall at her back. She sure hoped Dane would stop by like he'd done every night that week.

Caleb stalked toward her, a knife in his hand.

"Oh shit," she murmured as she curled her fingers tighter around the candlestick, holding it like a baseball bat. Prepared to swing, she tried to remain calm as he stalked closer.

The knife flashed and he hit her in the head with the handle as Rufus bit his ankle. "Fucking mutt," he mumbled as he kicked out at the dog.

She dropped to her hands and knees as the world wavered in and out.

"I don't want to hurt you, stupid girl," he mumbled as he stepped away from her.

A knock at the door had her screaming, hoping whoever it was would hear her. "Help me!" she screamed.

With a bang, the door flew open and there stood Dane. The room was spinning, so Vi mumbled, "Thank God," and sank down to lay on the floor to make it stop.

"What the…"

Caleb took off down the hall toward whatever window he'd broken to get in.

Dane ran after him, cursing when Caleb slipped out the window and took off. He hurried back into the living room, dropping to his knees in front of her.

"Vi, honey, don't move." Phone in hand, he dialed 911, his hands shaking as he relayed the info to the dispatcher and requested the sheriff put out an APB. Before he could dial Logan's number, he heard a siren approaching.

Dane watched as Vi put a hand to the cut on her head, her eyes going wide at the blood.

"Just lay still, an ambulance is coming." He pulled off his shirt and pressed it to the cut on her temple.

She looked up at him, wondering why he looked so pale and shaky. "Did you get him?"

"Slimy bastard got away. James will put out an APB. They'll find him." He brushed the hair away from her face with a shaking hand. "You let me worry about him."

"Violet!" Logan yelled before running into the house, stopping suddenly when he spied Dane kneeling on the floor in front of her, his shirt pressed against the bleeding wound at her temple.

"Vivi, honey? What happened?"

Dane looked up at him. "Later. James is on it."

Logan paced the length of the room and back, hurrying to the door when he heard another siren.

When he returned, the EMTs were right behind him. "She's in here."

As they checked her over, he called Cassie and told her everything was okay but to meet them at the hospital."

They had her on the gurney and ready to go when Logan's radio crackled.

James's voice came through. "No sign of the perp."

"Jesus, this is bringing back some bad memories," Logan muttered, following the EMTs pushing the gurney toward the door. He looked at Dane. "I'm riding in the ambulance." He tossed his keys to Dane. "Keep an eye on Steve until he's finished. I don't want there to be any mistakes gathering evidence. And grab a shirt out of my bag in the trunk."

The worried look on Logan's face stopped Dane's argument. Yeah, he loved Vi, but Logan was her father and that trumped any other relationship.

"I'll be there as soon as I can," Dane called to him before they closed the ambulance doors. With a whoop of the siren, they took off for the hospital.

Dane

He pulled on the shirt and tugged at the sleeves. His arms strained the shirt's fabric to its limit. He stepped through the door into the bedroom where Caleb had entered by breaking the window. Dane resisted the urge to grab the fingerprint powder from the deputy and do it himself. *What is taking him so long?* He needed to get to the hospital and check on Vi.

Rufus howled as the sound of another siren screamed in the quiet neighborhood.

James pulled up and parked alongside Logan's car. "You're still here?"

"Logan wanted me to keep an eye on the deputy. I called Dan, and he's on his way with some plywood to cover the broken window."

James studied him, his eyes taking in the ill-fitting shirt. "Wardrobe issue?"

"I used my shirt as a bandage. This one's Logan's." Dane swallowed hard, willing the nausea back.

"Oh, I see how it is. You're in love with her."

"Yeah. I guess I am. Have been since I was seven." They'd just started talking again this week and their relationship felt new and fragile, even though it began eighteen years ago. They had so much time to make up for, and now this.

"Go, I'll take care of the crime scene. Steve and I will clean up. Rufus can come to the station with me."

Dane ran a hand through his hair, hating that Vi's house was a crime scene. "Thanks."

Why the hell had Caleb broken into the house with Vi there? What could he have possibly wanted?

Now that James was on scene, he could finally leave for the hospital. He called Logan to get the latest as he hurried to the car. "Is she okay?"

"She's okay. Doc says there's no sign of concussion."

He let out a long breath, relieved that Vi would be okay. He still needed to get to the hospital and see for himself.

Even knowing it was against regs, he flipped on the lights and siren and sped toward the hospital to check on his girl.

Chapter Eleven

VIOLET

Flashlight app on, she held her phone in one hand and rummaged in the coat closet with the other. Rufus stood behind her and growled. Caleb had said something about a book he was after. What was so important about a book that he would break in and attack her for it?

"Yes!" she cried when she moved the box of hats and gloves to find a book lying flat on the floor beneath it. Book in hand, she carried it to the couch and set it on the coffee table.

In the light, the book looked old—like antique old. No title on the cover, she opened it to discover it was full of handwritten pages. They looked like recipes, but the ingredients weren't for anything she'd want to eat. The first called for bat's blood and the ash from a Beltane fire.

She flipped through the pages and stopped when she saw a pentagram. Dropping the book, she stood and backed away from the table. "Holy shit, these are spells." A breeze ruffled her hair and she turned to find the source. "What the…?"

Avoiding the end of the table where the book lay, she picked up her phone and retreated to the kitchen, Rufus following her.

She needed Dane. His reassuring presence would help her get up the courage to check out the book further. It was Saturday and Dane would be at the gym, so she sent him a text before grabbing a bottle of water and her coat.

Her seat on the porch felt far enough away from the book. She didn't know why she was so freaked out about a book of spells. It wasn't like the book could cast a spell on its own. She stroked the dog in her lap, glad for the warmth of his body against her legs.

Dane's truck pulled into her driveway, and he hopped out. "What's wrong?"

"I found what Caleb was looking for. It was hidden in the coat closet."

He noticed her shivering. "Why are you out here in the cold?"

"It looks like a really old spell book. I got kinda freaked out, so Rufus and I came out here."

He pulled her into a hug and she buried her face in his coat, her arms going around his waist. "Mmm…you're nice and warm."

"Let's get you in the house." He took her hand and led her in through the door. "Where is it?"

"On the coffee table. It just felt so creepy."

He took off his coat and she practically drooled at the sight of him in a pair of gray sweatpants and a tight tee shirt that showed off the size of his biceps.

"Seriously? You texted me because you were totally freaked out, but now you're ogling me like one of the muffins at Cassie's store?" he asked with a grin.

Her cheeks immediately heated, "Oops, sorry. Can't help it."

"Let's take a look at this spell book of yours."

The book didn't seem nearly so creepy with Dane sitting next to her. She opened the book and found the name 'Reverend Jake' scrawled inside the front cover. *Why does that name sound so familiar?*

Paging through the book, she stopped at a random page and tried to decipher some of the writing. The ink had faded to dull brown making it hard to read. "Possession?" she squinted at the page. "Yep, that says possession," she whispered. With a shiver she dropped the book and scooted closer to Dane.

"What?"

"That's says possession…" her brain whirled as she remembered why the Reverend Jake sounded so familiar. "Oh my God, this can't have belonged to *that* Reverend Jake, could it?" She muttered to herself.

"What's wrong Vi?"

"You remember the story of how my mom met my dad? The Rev who was after her?"

"Yeah, why?"

"I think this spell book belonged to him."

Later that afternoon, Logan and Dane were on the porch discussing the situation. Cassie sat next to Violet and stared at the book, her eyes unfocused as she remembered the demon the Rev summoned and the hell it wreaked on their lives.

"Those glowing green eyes," Cassie mumbled. "I'll never forget how they looked shining out of James's face. Demon's eyes." She shivered, rubbing her hands up and down her arms.

"Mom? You okay?"

"Yeah, I just don't like to remember all that. It was horrible to live through, and your dad almost died."

"He did? I don't remember you telling me that part. In fact, I don't remember you mentioning a demon at all."

"We just wanted to forget. It was so scary."

Violet stared at the name written in the book. "Why would Caleb have this?"

Logan walked into the room followed by Dane. "Good question. I think it's time Dane and I did some more digging on that ex-fiancé of yours."

Chapter Twelve

VIOLET

Even though she'd done hundreds of live shows, she was nervous. She'd gone ahead and signed a contract with Sky's The Limit Records and had recorded her very first single. Tonight was its official debut, and she knew the hometown crowd would love it because it was her, but would they really love the *song*?

Guitar case in hand, she locked the door behind her and gasped at the limo parked in front of her house. Colt LeBrea leaned against the front fender wearing his 'don't mess with me' face, partially hidden by his wraparound sunglasses.

"What is this?"

His demeanor changed in an instant, a smile lighting up his face. "Well, Adam wanted to surprise you. Wanted you to feel like the superstar you are about to become." He removed his sunglasses and motioned to the car. "Too much?"

She laughed. "In the best way."

He strode up her sidewalk and took her guitar case. "Stars don't carry their own equipment."

"I'm not a star."

"I heard your song. You will be soon." He held out his arm and escorted her to the car door which opened as they approached. "Working for Adam all these years I've heard a lot of bands and artists. You're going to be up there with the best of 'em."

She grinned, even though she was miffed at her uncle for that. He'd promised he wouldn't play the song for anyone until after she debuted it at the dance.

Dane stepped out and she almost sighed out loud as she looked him up and down. They'd just talked through some of their issues, and they were friends again, but seeing him in those black jeans paired with a dress shirt and suit jacket? Wowza. He sure cleaned up good.

Dane held out his hand to help her into the car. Growing up around Adam, she'd had her share of rides in a limo, but this was the first time the limo was for her.

Scooting across the seat, she made room for Dane. They were reconnecting, first as friends but hopefully it would grow into more. After she'd found out about the whole misunderstanding about why he left, she'd let her true feelings come to the surface. She wanted to be more than friends, that was for sure.

As the car left the curb, Dane took her hand. "I'm excited to hear your song."

She'd played bits and pieces of it for him while she was working on it but not the whole song. The snippets she'd played didn't have any lyrics that gave away the fact it was about him. "I hope you'll like it. It's scary, debuting something that could change my life."

He pulled her into a hug as the car stopped. "You got this, Vi. Pretend it's just you and me at your house. You're never nervous when we do that."

She looked down as she stepped out of the car and looked up to find her father standing there with her uncle. A death grip on his hand, she dragged Dane with her as she ran to her father. "Daddy!"

"Hey Vivi, you ready? Marie scheduled you first so you can enjoy the rest of the dance."

Colt appeared with her guitar case. He flipped open the clasps and held it out to her so she could grab the instrument. "Give me a sec to tune up and I'll be ready." She took a seat and hoped they couldn't see her hands shaking. She shouldn't be this nervous, but she was.

Her voice wobbled a bit. "All tuned up and ready to go."

Adam disappeared through the curtain and she heard the crowd applaud, thinking he was going to play.

"Sorry to disappoint you all but I'm not the one going to sing. I'm here to introduce Sky's The Limit Records' newest artist. She's got a brand-new song that's releasing tomorrow, but she's debuting it tonight for you. Now, I know you'll all recognize Fairfield Corners very own Violet Miller."

The crowd clapped enthusiastically, hooting and hollering. She took a seat on the stool placed at center stage in front of the drum kit. She reached out and slightly adjusted the height of the microphone.

"Hey everyone. This is something I wrote about coming home. I hope you like it."

She strummed the guitar and started to sing.

After she strummed the last chord and the music died away, the crowd was silent. *Oh shit, they hate..."*

As if released from a spell, they clapped and hooted and hollered even louder than before. She was glad they all seemed to like it but there was only one person's opinion she really cared about—Dane's.

She could feel the vibration of someone walking across the stage but couldn't hear them due to the crowd noise. She looked up to find Dane standing in front of her, a look on his face she wasn't sure she'd ever see again. The last time she'd seen that look was when they were at the Island just before her dad had shown up.

He took her guitar by the neck, unhooking the strap. His other hand pulled her to her feet and plastered her against him. The crowd hushed, waiting to see what would happen.

He kissed her. Short and sweet, certainly not nearly enough to suit her, but they'd just repaired their friendship and it was too soon for anything more than that.

"You like it then?"

He laughed heartily. "Of course, I do. You think I don't know it's about you and me?"

"Well…" She ran her hand up and down his arm. "I've had so many unrealized feelings I had to let them out somehow."

So focused on him and his reaction, she hadn't realized the crowd was silently staring at them.

He leaned down and whispered, "Um, we're the center of attention."

Red crept up her cheeks. "Oh, um, thanks everyone," she said into the mic. Dane leaned over and said, "Be sure to get your copy tomorrow!" And then she followed him off the stage.

The band hurried out from the wings, and she was surprised to see the lead singer was someone she knew. "Brandon? What are you doing here?"

"Your uncle saw us playing one of the open mic nights back in Philly. He signed us a couple of weeks ago."

She rushed over and hugged him. "That's awesome!" She turned to find Dane frowning at her, his hands shoved in his pockets. "Dane, come here and meet Brandon and the guys. We met at an open mic night a couple of years ago."

Dane walked over and grudgingly held out his hand. "Nice to meet you," he grumbled.

"This is Brandon and his husband, Kurt," she said as she smacked his arm. "Quit being all jealous."

His frown evaporated. "Really?" He cleared his throat with a rueful smile. "It's nice to meet you. Any friends of Violet's…"

Brandon kissed her cheek. "We'll have to catch up before we head back in a couple of days."

"Absolutely. Just let me know when you have some free time, I'll show you all the local sights."

Dane

His gut twisted when Vi ran up to the singer and reached up for a hug. *Did I misread her song that much?*

The blood pounding in his ears almost drowned out her voice when she introduced him and his husband. *Geez, I need to get a grip.* He was so close to having her back and he was acting like a jealous asshole.

He watched as Vi stowed her guitar back in its case and turn back to him. "What was that all about?"

"Can we find somewhere a bit more private to talk about this?" he asked, noting the crowd's attention was still on them.

Waving at her dad, she grabbed his hand and pulled him to the ladies' room. Pushing him through the door, she closed it behind them and flipped the lock.

Once they were alone, she turned to him, hands on her hips. "What the hell, Dane? We've only just become friends again and you want to act like a jealous boyfriend?"

He stared at her, dumbfounded. "Maybe because that's what it feels like. I know we've just repaired our friendship, but my feelings don't care it's too fast. All those feelings I thought had died came rushing back as soon as I saw you in that ridiculous little car of yours. They weren't gone, just dormant."

He ran his hands through his hair and stared back at her. "It took me years to get past those feelings, to learn how to ignore them—then one look at you, and *wham*. I'm a goner."

She reached up and put her hand on his face. "I can understand that."

"I don't know if I can *be* just your friend, Vi. I need for us to be more than that."

Chapter Thirteen

DANE

As Dane showered and shaved while getting ready for his evening with Vi, he let his mind wander back to where it all began—when his dad had kidnapped Bette and the Millers had taken him in to foster—and meander forward to the evening to come. Over the years, Cassie and Logan had asked him many times if he wanted them to adopt him. He'd refused, every time. He didn't want them to be responsible if what happened to his dad was hereditary. Scared of mental illness, he obsessively analyzed any errant thoughts.

His relationship with Vi had evolved slowly, over the course of many years. Dane remembered that it started turning into something more when he was sixteen. He'd shoved his feelings for Vi into the back of his mind, but they were always there...taunting him: *She never wrote, she doesn't love you, you don't deserve her...*

Now, he was going on an actual date with his Vi. He wiped his hands nervously on his pants, his palms damp and clammy. *God, this is the first time I've ever been this nervous before a date.*

Pinpointing the moment when his feelings started to change was hard, but he vividly remembered the moment he realized he loved her as more than a friend—the afternoon she beamed at him after putting an ivy ring on her finger. He swore he could almost see musical notes floating above her head amid swirls of green and blue, the same shade of blue as her eyes. Those eyes....*I could fall into them and stay there forever*. Deep, bottomless pools that promised so much, but he wasn't sure he could match the depth of passion he saw there.

They had spent so much time together and were considered practically inseparable from that first day on the porch steps. Afraid to make some real friends at first, he'd clung to Vi who, even at four years old, had an eternal, bright outlook on life. She was an old soul, and he often felt such a kinship with her that he wondered how he'd gone through life before he met her. Always a loner, he'd never really made any friends.

As he grew up, he finally made some friends, especially in high school. It was hard not to bond with his football teammates because they spent a lot of time together between practices and games. But the highlight of each game was always hearing Vi's voice in the crowd, first as a fan and then as a member of the band. He laughed when he realized he loved a band geek. It seemed sudden when it was time to decide what to do with his life beyond high school. He had to get a job, one that would support him. College was out. His grades stunk because he couldn't be bothered to study. He was too busy hanging out with Vi or listening to her latest song. God, she was talented. And her voice? He could listen to her all day, and sometimes he did.

Seven years earlier...

Boot camp had chewed him up and crapped him out an Army MP. He'd hefted his bag onto his shoulder and made his way to the parking lot, waiting anxiously for mail call every day. He'd gotten letters from Cassie and an occasional one from Logan, but never one from Vi. He wondered if she was still mad that he hadn't told her he was leaving.

Once the graduation ceremony ended, he'd spotted Logan waiting for him, leaning against the fender of his truck. As soon as he saw Dane he grinned. "So how does it feel to be an MP?" he asked, tossing Dane's bag into the back seat.

"I'm just glad that's over." He slipped into the passenger seat. "Where's Cassie?"

"She's riding back with Adam and Ragan. They left just after the ceremony so she could get stuff ready for the party tonight."

He wanted to ask about Vi but something stopped him. Rubbing his hands on his fatigues he asked about the party instead. "I hope it's not something big. I'd be happy with a family dinner and Cassie's spaghetti."

"Now, you know Cassie is way too excited for that." He laughed as he turned out onto the highway.

Dane ran his hands over the stubble of hair on his head, almost afraid to ask. "So, how is Vi?"

Logan frowned. "She still hasn't written? What is wrong with that daughter of mine?"

Dane shrugged. "We'll get it worked out while I'm home."

Another frown from Logan. "About that.… A last-minute spot opened up at that exclusive music high school she's been wanting to attend. She left yesterday."

Balling his fists, he wanted to scream in frustration. "Dammit," he muttered under his breath. *Getting a last-minute spot just when he was coming home for leave? This has to be a coincidence, right?* He sighed and stared out the windshield. "Okay, well, tell her… Never mind." He wouldn't let Vi's absence ruin his leave. He'd received his assignment and, when he got back, he was headed to Germany for at least two years.

The rumble of the tires on the highway lulled him to sleep and he woke up when he felt the truck slow for a turn. He blinked sleep out of his eyes and saw the outskirts of Fairfield Corners. He was home, but it wouldn't be the same without his Vi.

Over the next six years Vi had been somewhere else every time he'd returned home. First it was the special music high school, and then it was college in Philadelphia. A guy could get a complex…

And then he was free, his time in the Army finally over. That last few years he'd been stationed at Fort Knox in Kentucky. Even when he'd gotten his discharge papers, he'd waited to call Cassie and Logan —he wanted to surprise them. The motor in his '69 Camaro rumbled as he waited for the stoplight to change. He was so close, and wanted nothing more than to start his civilian life. He parked in the lot at the bookstore and shut off the car. He sat there, wondering what was next in his life. He hoped he could get a job as a police officer, maybe do the state police academy.

It had been a long two days' drive home. First, he'd driven the loaded up rental truck from Kentucky to Fairfield Corners, a tow dolly hooked to the back for his car. After he unloaded the truck and turned it in at the rental place, he gassed up his car and headed for Pennsylvania. He drove all day and most of the night, only stopping for a quick nap in a rest area. He made it to the graduation ceremony just in time to see Vi walk across the stage to receive her degree in music therapy. He hung back after the ceremony, watching as she received hugs from Cassie, Logan, and the rest of the family. He wanted nothing more than to walk over and give her a hug too, but her silence over the last seven years had made it clear that she didn't want to see him. Obviously, her feelings for him had changed even though he still felt the same way about her. His heart had felt like it would burst with pride as she'd walked across the stage, receiving her degree with top honors.

Before the crowd started to disperse, he'd hurried to his car and driven back to Fairfield Corners, telling himself he needed to get his stuff unboxed and put away in his apartment. Maybe the physical activity would help him forget that Vi would soon be in the same town, where he would have to see her every day and not be able to touch her.

That night, he fell into bed completely exhausted, his sleep only broken by dreams of Vi.

The next day…

The bell over the door jingled and he heard Cassie's voice coming from the office. "I'll be there in just a…" She looked up and squealed, "Dane! Your home!"

She ran up and pulled him into a hug. "Why didn't you let us know you'd be home? I need to call Ragan and get everyone together for a welcome home celebration."

He yawned, still tired from the last few days of driving. "That's okay, I don't want a party or anything."

"Well, that's just too bad. You be at the house by six tonight or you'll be answering to me, buster."

He grinned and pulled her in for another hug. "Thanks. You know I love you, right?"

"Of course, I do." She pulled her phone out of her pocket and started scrolling through her contacts. "You look tired. Go take a nap and I'll get things set up for tonight. Don't forget, six o'clock sharp."

"Okay, okay. I'll be there."

"Dane McWilliams, when did you get home?"

He turned to find Bette Fairfield standing in the archway between the bookstore and Bette's Beautiful Things. "Get over here and give me a hug."

He smiled huge and strode over to her, picking her up and hugging her tight. "I missed you."

She held him at arms-length for a once-over. "Are you home for good?"

With a smile he answered, "Yeah. Now I have to figure out what to do with the rest of my life."

"And I have no doubt you will do just that. Now, I want to know why you didn't tell anyone you were coming home."

"I didn't want to take anything away from Vi's graduation. I'm surprised Cassie doesn't have a huge party planned."

"You don't know? I would have thought Cassie would have told you."

"Told me what? Is something wrong?" His stomach did a weird flip at the thought of something being wrong with Vi.

"No, nothing's wrong. Vi isn't here. She's staying in Philly for the summer to work on a big concert. I guess she's going to be one of the headliners."

The message on his phone pinged, bringing him out of his reverie. He glanced at the clock, surprised to see it was almost time for him to go pick up Vi. He'd been lost in his memories for over an hour. He'd better get a move on, or he'd be late for their first date.

Chapter Fourteen

VIOLET SLOUCHED DOWN in the tub and let the hot water lap at her chin, a myriad of thoughts racing through her mind. It had been so long since she'd allowed her childhood memories of Dane to invade her thoughts. For years, she'd pushed them down, not wanting to torture herself. The memories were so vivid, even the ones from when he'd first come to stay with them when she was only four. His song had been so dark at first.

She'd found him sitting on the front steps, his music swirling madly. After plopping down on the step next to him she'd asked, "Watcha doin'?"

He'd stared straight ahead. "Just thinking."

She stared at the dark music whirling above his head became a bit lighter. "'bout what?"

"Living here," he blurted with a frown.

Unfazed, she'd studied his face. "Don't you like it here?"

"Yeah, too much. I'm afraid I'll have to leave."

"I won't let them send you away. Your song is already getting brighter."

His confused look made her smile. She'd tried to explain it to him the night before, but he didn't really understand how she could see music. She may have been only four, but she could tell he was only nodding like he understood just to make her feel better.

She scooted closer to him until her hip touched his. The warmth of her song spread from her hip into him. He'd tried to jerk away but the warmth somehow bound them together.

He watched as she paged through the book she'd brought out with her. He asked, "Do you feel that?"

"Yeah, your song needs more happy, so mine is helping."

He shook his head, but she knew he would understand one day.

The memory morphed into another day, when she'd been crying as Cassie checked Dane's clothes one more time. "I'm sorry, baby girl, but Dane has to go to school. We talked about this."

"I want him to stay here with me." Her bottom lip stuck out in a pout.

"I'll be home later, I promise," he said as he squatted in front of her. "If I don't go to school, they'll take me away."

She sniffed and wiped her face. "They will? Then you better go. I don't want them to take you away."

The alarm on her phone chimed, reminding her it was time to get ready. Once she was dressed, she dug around in her jewelry box, looking for the ivy ring he'd given her when she was thirteen. Then she remembered, she'd given it to him to fix the week before he left. Wearing it every day had worn down the cheap metal and it had cracked so badly she'd been afraid she was going to lose it. He'd promised to fix it. Her heart lurched at the thought it might be gone forever. That reminded her of the day he'd given her the ring, her thirteenth birthday...

He'd wiped his hands on his jeans again as she'd opened her presents. Pulling out a special notebook and pens for her songwriting, she'd smiled at him.

"Thanks, Dane," she said and kissed him on the cheek.

"There's something else in there," he said with a shy smile, laughing when she dug around in the box.

"Ooh, it's so pretty," she cooed when she found the ring.

She slipped it on her finger and beamed at him. "It's perfect."

Seeing that ring on her finger had made her blush as she stared into the eyes of the boy she'd loved since she was four.

"It's cheap, so you may need to coat it with clear nail polish or it might turn your finger green."

"I don't care. I love it!"

He ran his hand through his hair and stood. "I, uh... I need to go do my homework," he'd blurted before running up the stairs and slamming the door to his room.

Her phone pinged with a notification. She checked the screen, shocked to discover Dane would be there in ten minutes. Hurrying through her makeup routine, she finished getting ready.

As she hurried down the stairs it dawned on her—*Oh shit, I'm going out to dinner with Dane.* They'd talked about the misunderstanding that had torn them apart for seven years, and they'd agreed to try going on a date. She watched him walking up the sidewalk after parking his truck in front of her house. Yes, she wanted to see if they still had those feelings, but it also scared the shit out of her. She'd only been fourteen when he left. *Will he find me lacking?* Her weird hippie style along with the seeing music thing usually drove away any suitors...except for Caleb, and now she knew why.

Dane was the man in black: Black leather jacket with the collar turned up against the cooler weather, black trousers, and a black button-down shirt. She felt slightly underdressed in her sixties-inspired dress. *At least he isn't wearing a tie.* It would have helped if he'd told her where they were going—he'd gone all secretive when she'd asked.

The door open in invitation, she turned to the coat closet and pulled her long duster off its hanger. She heard the squeal of the screen door and then he knocked. "Come on in, Dane," she called as she searched the living room for her phone.

"You ready, Vi?"

"Just need to find my phone. Oh wait, I left it upstairs. Be back in a sec." Hurrying down the hallway, she berated herself for being so nervous. "It's just Dane, for heaven's sake. You've known him since you were four," she mumbled to herself. That was true, but it had also been seven years since they'd had any kind of friendship.

Grabbing her phone off the charger, she hurried back to the living room, slowing when she caught sight of him looking at her wall of photographs. There were a few up there that included him.

"I remember this one," he said pointing to a picture of the two of them in bathing suits, his arm over her shoulder. She was looking up at him in adoration as he stared straight into the camera. "That was out at the quarry that day the air conditioning broke down. Logan drove us out there to cool off."

Her face warmed as she remembered how she'd felt watching him in his bathing suit. She'd been thirteen and her feelings for him had started to change from hero worship to something more. "Yeah." Her mind wandered back to that day, the way the breeze ruffled his just-a-little-too-long hair. Back then, he'd always needed a haircut. "That's when my feelings started to change," she said without thinking.

He looked at her in shock. "You were only thirteen, and I was sixteen. God, no wonder Logan made me promise…"

"Promise what?"

He ignored her question and picked up her coat, holding it out for her to slide her arms in the sleeves. "We need to get going."

That was weird, wonder what that was about? She followed him out to the car, looking at him in surprise when he opened the passenger door for her and then closed it once she was settled into the seat.

Once he was in the truck, she commented," Oooh, such good manners."

"Your mom gave me a crash course in being a gentleman today, whether I wanted it or not," he said with a laugh. "It did keep me from talking myself out of the date," he admitted. "It's been seven years, what if those feelings aren't there anymore?"

"I don't think that's going to be a problem."

He pulled into the parking lot of The Corner Pub.

"The Pub?"

"Oh, I didn't think. You've been singing here. We can go somewhere else."

"No, it's fine. I'm just surprised you wanted to take me on a date where my family will be able to keep tabs on us."

"I guess I better be on my best behavior, then," he quipped.

They enjoyed good food, some great music, and her uncle kept his distance. The conversation stayed light—mostly they caught up on the last seven years. Some, he'd heard from Cassie and Logan, but a lot from the years while she was away at college was new to him. They avoided any mention of Caleb or the search for him.

He held her hand as they walked out to his truck. "I'm not ready for this to be over yet."

She cleared her throat. "I'd like to see your apartment."

He looked away and then stared into her eyes. "It's small, but it's enough for me."

She smiled. "You can tell a lot about someone from their space."

"Okay, but next time we'll go to your place."

It was only a couple of blocks from The Pub to his apartment over the bookstore. Pulling around to the back of the building, he parked close to the door. She waited while he came around to open her door for her, and then he held her hand as he led her up the stairs. Stopping briefly to unlock the deadbolt, he opened the door with a flourish. "Welcome to my humble abode."

She stepped into the room and just stared, trying to take in every detail. All one room but separated into three distinct areas. In the front, there was a comfy looking couch and a big-screen television with a shelf of stereo equipment for the living area. Against the far wall was a small section of cabinets with a stove, fridge, and a small café table with two chairs for the kitchen. And in the far corner, the bed. With a blush she took off her coat and draped it over one of the chairs.

"Come, sit. Let's talk some more." With his hand at her back, he guided her to the couch. "How about a beer? I wasn't expecting to have you here tonight, so I don't have any wine."

"A beer sounds good," she said as she picked up the book he'd been reading.

He handed her a beer and sat next to her, turning slightly to watch her.

"I have to be honest…having you here in my space? The urge to kiss you is getting harder to ignore."

Looking at him through her lashes she replied, "Same."

"Oh, thank you God," he said before he pulled her close and kissed her. With a groan his hand went to the back of her neck to hold her closer.

Her sigh wiggled down his spine and into his toes, all the blood in his body headed for his groin. *She is actually here in my apartment, letting me kiss her.*

She sat back and watched his eyes—his pupils blocked out most of the color, making them look almost black. Taking a deep breath, she whispered, "I, uh, need a minute."

He pointed to the bathroom door. "Through there." He used the time she was gone to do some deep breathing of his own, trying to calm down his libido. He finally had her in his apartment and didn't want to scare her off.

Violet

She stood at the sink and stared at her reflection. Her lips were puffy and red from his kisses, and her eyes were dark blue with desire, so dark they looked almost black.

She returned to the couch and sat on his lap, facing him. "I want you, Dane." Her heart sped up as his smile grew bigger.

"Really?"

She stood, watching Dane's chest rise and fall. He rose and stared into her eyes, unbuttoning his shirt and letting it fall to the floor. Her mouth watered at the sight—muscular arms (one covered in a vine-like tattoo), washboard abs, and the sexiest forearms she'd ever seen on a man.

She licked her lips as his head dipped toward hers.

Dane

God, she's gorgeous. The combination of her red hair and those deep blue eyes... He ran his fingers down her cheek, trailing them down her neck until they rested on the tops of her breasts. So close, his fingers practically itched to get under her shirt and touch her. As much as he wanted to grab the neckline of her dress and rip it, he stroked his hands down to her hips and finally to her thighs. Grabbing the fabric of the skirt, he pulled it up until he could feel the bare skin of her legs.

Her breaths became pants. *Good God, he hasn't even touched any of the important parts yet. I'm going to kill him if he doesn't hurry up.* Pulling her dress up over her head, he dropped it on the floor and swooped in for another kiss, nestling his cock against that little inviting space at the top of her thighs.

He stepped back and looked at her, now clothed in only a few scraps of lacey fabric. He breathed, "Oh Vi, you're so beautiful." Grabbing her hand, he walked her over to his bed. His fingers fumbled with the button and fly on his trousers, finally dropping them to the floor.

She reached out and touched his chest, the feel of her fingertips against his skin burned into his soul. *I've waited so long for this.* His muscles bunched at her every touch.

"Am I hurting you?" she asked, her eyes scanning his face.

"Only in the best way. I'm doing my damnedest not to throw you on that bed and ravish you right this second."

"I've never...what I mean is..." she looked away. "I've never really had any foreplay. Caleb—"

"Do *not* mention that asshole's name when we're being intimate," he growled. It took all of his will not to grab her and kiss every last memory of that dick away.

She stepped back and a tear rolled down her cheek. "O-okay," she stammered. She looked down at her feet. "I'm sorry."

"Fuck," he muttered. "Did he hurt you in bed?" He swallowed hard, the thought of someone hurting his Vi making him feel sick. He tilted her head back with a finger under her chin. "Did he force you?"

A shake of her head had him letting the air out of his lungs in a rush. "We can stop if you..."

"Oh, no. Nothing like that. He just never did anything to prepare me. A lick here, a suck there, and then he was pumping away. He never cared that my body wasn't ready for him." Her statement ended with a sob that tore right through him.

When he shot off the bed, she practically screamed, "No!" She stood and stroked down his chest. "I want this. I know you'll never hurt me."

Her statement cooled his temper. She was right—he'd cut off his own arm before he'd intentionally do anything to hurt her. "Okay then, let's start over. What happened in the past doesn't matter now. We're here together, finally."

His gentle hand cupped her neck and he kissed her, his other hand skimming her waist. Fingertips danced across his skin, raising goosebumps in their wake. His heartrate went through the roof as she explored his body, from his neck down to his navel. It took all his concentration to keep from taking her hand and placing it on his dick. God, her touch had him so hard it hurt.

"Touch me," she whispered, "please."

His hands shook as he skimmed his fingertips over her breasts, rubbing his thumbs lightly over the pebbled nipples. "So responsive," he muttered, licking his lips. He laid her on the bed and settled in between her legs. "Don't worry, you're in control Vi."

Using his tongue, he licked a path from her neck to her breasts before taking a nipple in his mouth and sucking while flicking it gently.

Her hips rose and she moaned. "I don't…"

One hand holding her breast in the perfect position for his tongue to play, his other hand inched down slowly until it was at the apex of her thighs. God, he wanted nothing more than to sink into her warmth, but this was about her and allaying her fears.

His fingers explored her folds, finding that little nub of nerves that was swollen and ready for his touch. Forming slow circles, his fingers dipped lightly into the wetness and back to that bundle until she writhed beneath him.

"Ahhhh, I…" she panted.

Sucking harder, his thumb circled her nub as another finger eased into her—and that was all it took. He felt the ripples begin, watching her face as her entire body tensed in orgasm. "So beautiful," he muttered, kissing her neck.

"Is it always like that?" she asked as he snuggled her ear with his nose.

"If you do it right," he replied with a snicker.

"What about you?" she asked. He grimaced when she wiggled. "Does it hurt?"

"Not really. I'm just so turned on by the sight of you coming apart for me."

She reached between them and ran her fingers along his cock. "Let's see if I can do the same," she said as she licked her lips.

Violet

She loved the satiny smoothness of his skin. Her girlfriends had told her stories about what pleased a man, she'd just never needed to try any of them out on her ex. Now, she licked her lips in anticipation of learning what Dane liked. Obviously, he was way more giving in the lovemaking department than that other asshole.

She took him in her hand, grinning when his breath caught in his chest. "Oh, you like that," she muttered as her hands explored. She leaned up and started at his nipples. She wondered if he would feel what she had when he'd sucked on hers. Only one way to find out...

Using her tongue, she licked at one of his nipples, loving how his hips moved when she did. With a grin, she licked around one and then the other, relishing how his breathing hitched and he panted.

When she hesitated, he growled, "Babe," and panted, "keep going."

Wondering what it felt like to suck on him. She did, and he groaned. "Give me a sec."

"Did I do it wrong?" she asked.

"No. I'm trying to think of anything but your mouth on me. You've got me so hard," he said as he took one of her hands and placed it on his dick, "I don't know how much more I can take."

"Oh, well, we can..."

He put his hands behind his head. "No, Vi. This is your time to play."

"But wouldn't it be better for you if we actually made love? Then, after, I can play."

With a growl, he flipped her onto her back and nuzzled her neck. "God, I love you woman."

A few strokes of his tongue on her nipples and she was writhing beneath him again. "Please, Dane, now."

Dane

Finding her as wet as before, he did what she asked. That first slide into her wet warmth, and he was gone. No control whatsoever. He vowed the next time he would take his time, but the tingling was already starting at the base of his spine. He stopped and panted in her ear.

She put her hands on his shoulders. "Why'd you stop?"

"I'm trying not to blow too early. I don't want this feeling to end."

Her legs wrapped around his hips and her heels dug into his back, pulling him further into her. With a groan, he let his body take over. A few slow strokes in and out and he came, hard, grinding himself into her. At his first groan, Vi's body responded by clenching around him, wringing out every drop of cum.

He kissed her, willing his heartrate to slow from its present gallop. Controlling his breathing, he traced the shell of her ear with his tongue.

Her reply was a delicious shiver.

"I didn't hurt you, did I?" If he'd hurt her at all, he'd never forgive himself.

"No, that was..." she hesitated as if searching for the correct word, and then breathed, "wonderful." With a goofy smile on her face, she pulled him down on top of her and hugged him tight.

She whispered, "I thought I was bad at sex. He told me I was worthless in bed."

He nuzzled her neck. "You are far from worthless."

She stiffened. "But was it really good?"

He rolled off her, laughing hard. "Were you not just there? I don't think I've ever cum so hard before. I saw stars."

"Oh, so it wasn't just me? I've never..." she laughed. "Shit, I've never had an orgasm like that before. Well, not *with* anyone. I mean, I've used a vibrator..."

He stopped her words by kissing her. "No more talk about vibrators, it's making me hard again already. You're gonna kill me." He went into the bathroom and returned with a wet washcloth, using it to clean between her legs and his cock. "Ready for round two?" He tossed the used washcloth towards the bathroom door.

"Oh goody. My turn to play." With an evil grin, she kissed her way down his body until her mouth found his dick and she tried out all those ideas.

Violet woke to the sun streaming across her face. That wasn't right, her bedroom window was across the room from the foot of her bed. A warm weight across her stomach had her opening her eyes with a smile. Oh, yeah. Dane. Sex. *No, it was more than that.* They'd made love all night. Stretching her arms above her head, she looked over to find Dane watching her.

"Sleep well?" he asked with a grin. His hair stuck up in spikes and his cheeks were covered in stubble. He looked positively yummy.

"Yeah. Now I need to, umm, use the bathroom."

He moved his arm and watched as she stood, the sheet dropping away as she padded to the bathroom.

He was up and filling the coffee maker when she came out. Bold as you please, she walked over to his dresser and opened a few drawers until she found what she was searching for. Pulling one of his tee shirts over her head, she let it settle down over her hips. A quick search of the floor, and she pulled on her panties.

Wishing she had her yoga mat, she moved the coffee table to make room for her morning Asanas. She started with some stretching and bent to touch her toes.

She giggled when Dane groaned, "God, woman, you trying to kill me?" He watched the coffee brew for a moment before he hurried over to the bathroom. "I need a shower," he mumbled, slamming the door behind him.

Running through an abbreviated routine, she was sitting at the table and sipping her coffee when he walked out of the bathroom, steam rolling out of the small room.

Dressed only in sweats, she watched as he padded back to the kitchen, his bare feet slapping against the wooden floor.

"You want some breakfast? I think I have some bacon left."

"Huh?" she looked up at him. She'd been too busy watching the way his glutes flexed when he'd bent over to peer into the fridge.

"Bacon? Breakfast?" he asked with a grin.

Her cheeks heated as she nodded. "You're certainly more...um...muscular than you were in high school."

He barked out a laugh. "Oh, so that's what's got you so flustered this morning."

"Oh, shut up. I saw the look on your face when you took my dress off last night. I'm guessing the feeling is mutual."

A pack of bacon in one hand and a couple of eggs in the other, he kissed her on top of the head. "Oh yeah, it sure is." He got a frying pan out of the cupboard, carefully laying down the strips. As the bacon sizzled, he readied the bread for toasting and got the butter out of the fridge.

Vi sat and watched him cook, enjoying how his muscles smoothed and bunched as he moved. *Why did I ever think I was in love with Caleb?* It had always been Dane. Even through the guilt, she'd always hoped it would one day come to this.

They sat in silence as they ate, both of them lost in their own thoughts, their hands entwined under the table. Together, as it always should have been.

After breakfast, Vi had showered and was searching for her shoes. "As much as I want to spend the day with you, I'm supposed to be covering a shift for Mom in about an hour. Dad's got the day off, and I think she wanted some alone time with him." She picked up one shoe and scanned the room for the other. "Do you see my other shoe?"

"No, maybe it's under the couch."

She got down on her knees and bent over to check. She stood, her cheeks flushed from exertion. "Well, crap. It's not here."

Leaning against the counter, Dane let the shoe dangle from his fingers by the ankle strap. "Oh, look what I found. What'll you give me for it?"

"You just wanted to see me with my butt in the air," she laughed as she stalked toward him and grabbed her shoe. Steadying herself on the barstool, she strapped on one heel and then the other.

"Why do you wear those things? They look so uncomfortable."

"They aren't, really. I'm used to them." She winked. "Besides, they make my butt look amazing." She slapped his hand away as he reached out to touch said butt. "No time for that. I've got to get home, change, and get back here. And I'm sure Rufus needs to go out." She looked down at her feet, wanting to say the words aloud but afraid it was too soon. They'd only just started dating, after all.

"What is it?" he asked, pulling her closer. "You know you can tell me anything, right?"

The apprehension in his eyes had her blurt, "God, it feels too soon to say this… I love you, Dane."

He relaxed. "Oh. Is that all?"

She hit his arm. "Is that all? Conceited much?"

"Owww," he whined as he rubbed his arm, smiling. "Girl, I've loved you since I was seven years old. Why would you be afraid to tell me you feel the same?"

"Well, maybe because, until a couple of weeks ago, I thought you hated me. Saying it out loud is a huge deal for me."

"Never be afraid to tell me how you feel." He kissed her until her toes curled, and then he gently eased her away from him. "Now go, before I rip that dress off of you and show you just how much I love you." He laughed as she wobbled a bit.

"Promises, promises," she called as she walked out the door.

Chapter Fifteen

One week later

VIOLET

She struggled against the ropes binding her hands behind her back. Caleb stood within a circle drawn on the floor with what looked like white sand.

"Why are you doing this?"

He turned his dark eyes to hers. "My grandfather, the Rev, believed the demon would bring power to the person who called him from the depths of the other side. The Rev almost did it until your dad stopped him with the help of your great-grandmother's ghost."

"Why me?"

He bent and lit the fire he'd laid. Flames reflected in his eyes as he stared at her. "You're the direct descendent of the one in the prophesy. Killing you should be enough to bring forth the demon. The stories have been passed down in my family and we will finally get what's coming to us for our devotion."

The urge to scratch off the upside down cross he'd marked on her forehead with a black paste intensified. The mark began to smoke, the haze burning her eyes. "Make it stop," she cried as she tried to use her shoulder to brush off the mark.

"Oh, calm down. It won't be long, now. Soon, it will be time for the sacrifice and the green-eyed demon, Helagong, can be called forth."

She struggled harder, praying that Dane and her dad would find her in time. The air swirled with magic, and she began to see wisps of music. *What does this mean?*

As Caleb chanted, the wisps gathered together and began to form swirls of a song, its melody starting to play in her head. "I hope I can use this against him," she mumbled to herself as she gathered the music to her. *Thank God, he didn't gag me*, she thought as the music swelled within her, until it could no longer be contained. She opened her mouth and the song erupted, flying through the sky and swirling around Caleb, tighter and tighter, until it held him immobile.

With one long note, the bonds holding her wrists and ankles parted and she was free. The tingle of blood flowing back into her extremities helped her to continue. Her voice rose on a high note and Caleb fell over, his eyelids fluttering.

Her ankles felt stiff but didn't buckle when she ran toward the door, crying out in frustration when it wouldn't open. Focusing the swirls of music at the door, she stepped back and pushed them through it, smashing it to smithereens.

Her energy depleted, she stumbled out the door and stared at the stone stairs in front of her. Knees trembling with the effort, she slowly climbed each step, forcing herself up and out of the chamber of horrors. With a cry of relief, she pushed open one final door and she was out in the open. Dropping to her knees, she sat back and thanked whatever god had sent the music to save her.

The scrape of a shoe on stone made her jump up and look around wildly. *I have to get away...* The forest around her twittered with bird song and the rustling of wind-moved branches. *Which way do I go?* The glint of sun on a chrome bumper led her to the left. She stumbled out of the forest into a clearing where Caleb's car sat, waiting for its owner to return.

"Hopefully, he's dumb enough to leave the spare key hidden in the wheel well," she mumbled as she walked toward the vehicle, scanning the forest for any movement. The key was right where it was supposed to be, and she thanked God that Caleb was a dumbass and constantly locked his keys in the car. Come to think of it, that should have clued her in to who he really was instead of the mask he wore around her. He'd only let the mask slip after they were engaged and he'd mistakenly thought she'd go with the flow. Idiot.

Sliding into the car, she turned at the sound of a voice and saw Caleb running toward her.

"Oh crap!" she squeaked as she slammed the car door and started the engine. Shoving the shifter into drive, she stomped on the gas and held her breath until the tires gained some traction and the car shot forward. Following the faint ruts in the grass, she prayed they would lead somewhere she could find a phone. Dane was probably going ballistic trying to find her.

Dane

Vi hadn't picked up a call from him all morning, even ignoring his texts. That wasn't like her. Even if she was deep in the throes of a songwriting jag, she'd send him an emoji so he knew she wasn't just ignoring him. After a quick call to Logan, he was worried. They'd had no contact with her all day. His gut told him something wasn't right, and he'd learned to pay attention to it after it kept him from getting his ass blown up in a war zone.

He pulled out his phone and opened the tracking app he'd added on Vi's phone when they'd started spending so much time together.

Following the map on the app, he drove through town and stopped next to a corn field. That couldn't be right, the app said her phone was right here. He got out of the car and checked along the road, discovering a set of skid marks that veered toward the field and some broken down cornstalks. Following the tracks, he noticed some of the corn stalks had been propped up to hide the path that opened up in front of him now that he'd walked into the corn itself.

The glint of the sun on metal had his heart racing before he started running. Vi's car sat in front of him, the driver's door hanging open.

"Vi, honey?" he said as he walked closer, his stomach turning over on itself. The breeze rustling the corn stalks stopped, highlighting how deathly quiet it was. The car was empty except for her purse sitting on the passenger seat.

His senses alert and in full-on Army MP mode, he scanned the area as he pulled out his phone and called Logan.

When Logan answered, he barked out the information. "I found Vi's car. It's in a field out off County Road 47. It looks like someone tried to hide it."

He listened to Logan's curses, then replied, "Her purse is here," he mumbled as he dug through it, "and her phone. That's how I found the car, I tracked her phone." He listened again. "I'm worried. She wouldn't have left without her purse. I've got a gut feeling it was Caleb. That slimy bastard was playing her for some reason."

At Logan's instructions, he stayed and waited for the sheriff and a crime scene unit from Fort Wayne to arrive. He paced along the berm, fuming at having to wait. He wanted to be out there searching for her.

Once the sheriff showed up and he'd relayed everything he knew, he waited for James to give him the go-ahead to leave. He was on duty, and this was a crime scene, so he had to listen to his boss—no matter how much he knew he needed to keep searching.

James stopped his pacing by putting a hand on his shoulder. "Dane, we've got an APB out on Caleb and his car. We'll find her."

He could tell James was worried and that scared him. "Now tell me one more time, when was the last time you had any contact with Violet?"

"We had coffee together at the bookstore this morning before I came on shift at nine."

James's radio crackled and the dispatcher relayed that Violet had been found out past Woodview on the edge of the state park and had been taken to the hospital there.

Dane stared at James. "If you have more questions they'll have to wait." He ran to his car and took off in a hail of gravel and dust, with full sirens and lights.

"Thank God," he muttered under his breath as he sped down the highway. His heart pounded in his chest as he swerved around cars, willing his unit to go faster. The hospital meant she was hurt somehow.

He heard his name coming over the radio. "Dane, dammit, slow down. You won't do Violet any good if you're dead."

He checked his mirror and saw Logan right behind him. A quick check of his speedometer showed he was doing a hundred and ten. Easing his foot off the gas pedal, he let the car slow down to a reasonable speed—eighty. He wasn't willing to go any slower.

Luckily, the hospital was on this side of Woodview. He parked in one of the ER spots and took off for the entrance, Logan hot on his heels. His heart thumped so loudly in his ears he could hardly hear the clerk asking who he was there for.

Logan spoke up from behind him, "Violet Miller, she's my daughter."

"Right this way deputies, She's in curtain four."

Dane rushed past him, checking each curtained area until he saw her lying on a bed, eyes closed.

"Fuck," he whispered to himself as he had to remind his knees not to collapse. She looked peaceful, though as pale as the white pillowcase. As he pulled up a chair and sat next to her, he realized Logan had never questioned his extreme reaction to her disappearance.

Her pale hand in his, he looked up at his foster father. "I'm sorry. I broke my promise to you. I love her and that's never going to change."

Logan's brow furrowed in question. "What promise?"

The doctor stepped into the area and smiled. "Good, she's still sleeping." He checked the chart in his hand.

Dane didn't even look up, intent on watching the rise and fall of her chest.

Logan motioned for the doctor to follow him out into the hall. "What's her condition?"

"A few bruises and some rope burns on her wrists and ankles. Other than that, she's just exhausted. I'd like to watch her for a few more hours, just to be safe."

Overhearing their conversation, Dane relaxed a bit and kissed the back of Vi's hand.

"Thank God." Logan said as he pulled his phone out of his pocket. "Her mother will be relieved."

"Let me know if you have any questions. I'll be by in about an hour to check on her."

The doctor walked away, and Logan returned to the cubicle.

Logan picked up the blanket covering her feet and scowled at the rope burns. "Fucker's gonna pay for that," he muttered.

The Woodview sheriff poked his head into the cubicle. "Deputy Miller?"

"Yes, call me Logan. And this is Dane."

"I've got some questions for you. Can we talk somewhere more private?"

"Sure." They followed him to a break room.

"A camper found your daughter stumbling down a seldom used old logging road that borders the state park and called 911. We did a search and found an abandoned car that belongs to a Caleb Brighton."

"Motherfucker, I knew it was him," Dane ground out.

"So, you know this person?"

Logan rubbed the back of his neck. "My daughter's ex-fiancé."

"We found where the car had been driven out of the park through a meadow. An extensive search revealed an old underground bunker of some kind. We're trying to make sense of what we found there." He pulled some polaroid pictures out of the folder in his hand. "Your daughter doesn't remember being in the chamber or how she got free."

The pictures showed the fire that had still been burning and the salt circle, along with the pieces of the shattered door. The sheriff pointed to the remains of the door. "Any idea what could have done this?"

They both shook their head as they answered, "No."

"It exploded outward. You can see the fragments halfway up the staircase. Could your daughter have done this?"

"No. She's strong for her size, but that had to take a tremendous amount of strength."

"My deputies are still collecting evidence. We're keeping an eye out for Mr. Brighton. I'll keep you in the loop."

"Thank you," Logan replied as he shook his hand. "Appreciate it."

Logan went to follow the Sheriff back out into the hallway when Dane stopped him. "Let's talk about why you're not surprised that I declared my love for your daughter. I thought we'd been keeping it a secret. I wasn't sure how you were going to feel about the two of us being together since I made you that promise."

"That's the second time you've mentioned a promise. What promise?"

Dane walked over to the window and stared out at the parking lot, not wanting to face Logan while he confessed. "The day you took me to enlist in the Army, I promised you I would let her grow up and live her own life." He turned to find Logan looking at him quizzically.

"And how did you break this promise?"

"We've been seeing each other for a couple of months now, ever since she threw Caleb out."

A smile took over Logan's face, and he laughed.

Dane thrust his hands on his hips. "What's so damned funny?"

"You fulfilled your promise. You let her grow up and experience the world for herself. She's a grown woman now. She can love whomever she chooses. Besides, it's been obvious you two are together any time you're in the same room."

Dane crumpled into a chair, as if all the air had been let out of him. "God, I've been so worried that you'd be furious when you found out. Vi told me I was nuts for thinking that but…"

"Dane, after we took you in, I saw how you grew to care for each other and I hoped it would evolve into the true love I know you're capable of. Thinking of you and my daughter together makes me happy." He put his hand on Dane's shoulder. "When she introduced us to Caleb, I hated him on sight, I knew something wasn't right with him. You have any idea how hard it was for me to hold my tongue?"

"I can relate. The thought of that slimy creep's hands on her…" he balled his hands into fists wanting to hit something.

Logan slapped him on the back. "I'm sure you want to get back to Violet."

"Thank you."

"For what?" Logan asked.

"For having a daughter like Vi. And for molding me into a man that might one day be worthy of her love."

Logan smiled and walked away.

Violet

The steady beep of the monitor reassured her that she hadn't imagined escaping from Caleb. The cubicle was empty. She pushed herself up and rubbed her hands down her face. *Wow, I feel like I haven't slept in a week.*

Her body sagged, needing rest. She wondered where everyone had gone. She thought she'd heard Dane's voice whispering in her ear.

The sound of a throat being cleared made her look up. There stood a handsome dark-haired man that looked vaguely familiar.

"Uh, hello?"

"I just wanted to check that you were okay."

"And you are?" she asked.

"Oh, sorry. You were kind of out of it when I found you." He stuck his hands in his pockets. "I'm Jessie Monroe. I'm the one who found you stumbling along the old logging road."

"Thank you! I don't know how you found me but…"

Dane walked into the cubicle and took the chair next to the bed. "Who is this?" he asked grumpily.

"Behave," she told him with a smile. "This is the guy who found me, Jessie Monroe."

"You must be Dane." Jessie stepped forward with a slight limp. "She told me about you while we were waiting for the ambulance."

Dane stood and shook his hand as he scanned the stranger. "What branch?"

"Marines. You?"

"Army."

As they sized each other up another stranger peeked into the cubicle. "Hey Jessie, how's our girl doing?"

Dane frowned again. "Our girl? Who is this?"

Violet laughed. "Calm down, this is the EMT from the ambulance. I'm fine, Cam. Thanks for checking."

Dane stepped around the end of the bed to shake Cam's hand. "Thanks for helping MY girl."

Vi giggled. "So much testosterone," she muttered before a jaw-cracking yawn snuck up on her. "Oh, sorry, I'm still a bit tired."

"We'll let you get some sleep."

"Thanks guys, really," Dane said as they exited the area.

"What was that all about?" Vi asked before yawning again.

"Just me being an insecure ass. You feeling okay?"

"Yeah, just tired. Sit down, I'm getting a crick in my neck looking up at you."

He sat and took her hand, kissing the back of it.

"What's with the PDA? I thought we were keeping things secret for now?"

Dane squirmed in the chair. "Your dad and I had a talk while you were sleeping."

She yawned again.

"We'll talk about it later. Go back to sleep."

Gripping his hand tighter, she brought it up to her cheek. "Okay." She was asleep within moments, a smile on her face.

Chapter Sixteen

Four weeks later

DANE

He pored over the files spread out on the desk in front of him. Caleb was still at-large, and it was making him nuts. Why couldn't they find him?

"Well, shit," he heard coming from the sheriff's office. "Dane!"

James scowled at him from his seat behind the desk. "Come in and sit down."

They heard the dispatcher greeting Logan.

"Good, Logan should hear this too."

Logan walked into the office and looked from Dane to James. "What's happened?"

James pinched the bridge of his nose. "I was running a background check on Caleb, so I looked into his family." He leaned back in his chair and stared at Logan. "You better sit down. It took some doing, but we finally found Caleb's family."

"What is it?" Dane demanded.

"This won't mean anything to you, Dane, but it will to Logan." He turned the file in front of him around so the deputies could read the paper. "Caleb's grandparents were involved in a cult."

"God dammit! Not this shit again!" Logan thundered, as he jumped out of the chair to pace the length of the office. "I thought we were done with this."

Dane watched as Logan paced, muttering under his breath about green-eyed demons.

"I don't understand, what…"

Logan sat and put his head in his hands. "I don't know if I can do this again."

Dane looked from Logan to James and back again. "Will someone please tell me what the hell is going on?"

Logan gripped the arms of the chair so hard his knuckles were white before jumping up and pacing again.

James turned the file back around and closed it. "I'll explain everything, but you need to keep an open mind."

Scrubbing his hands over his face, Dane said, "Okay. I'll try."

"All this happened back when Logan first came to Fairfield Corners and Cassie had just returned to town to run her grandmother's bookstore. Strange things started happening. Doors unlocking themselves, objects disappearing and reappearing in odd places, things like that. Then Cassie started having nightmares about the night her ex-boyfriend attacked her."

Logan got up and walked to the door. He turned around and asked, "Either of you want coffee?" When they nodded, he left the room.

"He doesn't need to hear this, he lived it." James sipped from the bottle of water on his desk. "Cassie started getting creepy threats—ones that appeared when the bathroom mirror steamed up, things like that. I asked Logan to move in with Cassie to protect her until we could find out who was behind the threats. Now, at this point the two of them got on each other's nerves something fierce so it wasn't easy for either of them. Eventually, they both mellowed out a bit and, well, you know the rest of that. Cassie's ex showed up with some crazy story about his father, Reverend Jake, and his cult that worshiped a green-eyed demon. We didn't believe it at first, but the evidence started piling up. This demon tried to possess Logan so it could kill Cassie. It was convinced her death would allow it to return to this world permanently."

"You're kidding, right? This is some kind of joke?" Dane asked, though his gut told him it was the truth.

"It's true, all of it." He looked at Dane and continued, "Halloween night, Cassie's ex returned, possessed by the demon, and tried to kill Cassie after she'd closed the store for the night. Logan saved her and almost died in the process."

Dane rubbed the stubble sprouting on his cheeks, wanting the rasp of his hand against the hairs to reassure him. No such luck.

"So, Caleb's grandfather was part of this cult. That's where he got the book. The book of spells we found at the house."

"Yes, and he obviously believes he can call forth the demon again."

Dane hung his head and massaged the muscles in the back of his neck. "As crazy as this story sounds, my gut is telling me it's the truth."

"There's something about Fairfield Corners. Prophetic dreams, mystical music, people who can see ghosts and know things they shouldn't."

"Mystical music? You're talking about Vi, aren't you? How she can 'see' people's songs?"

He nodded, pursing his lips. "Yes, among other things."

"Other things?"

He ticked them off on his fingers. "Ragan sees what's going to happen; Faith and her ghosts; Adam and Ragan's song; Logan's dreams..." he tapped his thumb, "and Vi's sees people's 'songs'."

A crash made them both jump up and run out into the main office area where Logan stared at the shards of a coffee cup on the floor, coffee dripping down the wall.

"Sorry, James. I should have realized. I dreamt about that night earlier this week. I was hoping it was just the stress of him taking her. We should have told you kids the whole story, but we thought the demon was gone for good."

Logan grabbed a roll of paper towels and started mopping up the coffee from the wall. "Dane, first, you need to take the book and give it to Bette. And go ask Faith for her notes. Cassie told her everything and she fictionalized it. Having all the details will help you with the investigation."

Dane's eyes went wide, "Demon Undone? That really happened? I always wondered why Cassie wouldn't carry it in the bookstore."

"Some of it is true. Like I said, ask Faith. I'm sure she kept all her notes."

Driving across town, Dane turned the idea of demons being real around in his mind. Well, he knew witches were real, Bette was one. They'd given Caleb's book to Bette to have the local coven look it over. Bette Fairfield, the woman his dad went to prison for kidnapping, was one of his oldest friends. They'd bonded over the traumatic experience that brought them both to the small Indiana town.

As he drove out of Fairfield Corners, his mood brightened slightly when he saw the blue sky reflected in the water that filled the quarry, a popular swimming spot during the summer since it was closer than the lake.

He drove past the quarry and continued on toward her house, his mind going back to the first time he'd gone to Bette for comfort.

He'd been in Fairfield Corners for a couple of months when he couldn't stand the gossip anymore. He'd heard the whispers at school, the students parroting what they'd obviously heard from their parents.

"That's him. Bet he's as crazy as his father. Did you hear what he did?"

"Why don't they have him locked up somewhere?"

"What if he goes crazy here at school?"

By the end of the day, all he could think about was getting away. If he went home to the Miller's, Cassie would try to help but she didn't really understand. He needed to talk to Bette because she was the only one who did, but she lived in Fort Wayne.

If he couldn't see her, maybe just being by himself would help quiet the voice in his head that repeated everything he'd heard whispered about him at school. It was cool outside, so maybe he could ride out to the quarry. There wouldn't be anyone out there.

Pulling his bike out of the rack, he rode off in the opposite direction from home. It felt like he'd been pedaling forever when he finally saw the sign: Fairfield Brothers' Quarry. In smaller print below that: No lifeguard on duty—swim at your own risk. The parking lot was deserted, just as he'd hoped. Finally, he could be alone. Leaning his bike against the signpost, he trotted over to a large rock overlooking the pit. Aquamarine blue water sparkled in the sun, the breeze ruffling the surface. He pulled up his collar and put his back to the breeze, letting the sun warm his face.

As if a dam burst, the tears came hot and fast. He couldn't hold them back any longer.

"Hey, you okay?"

So absorbed in his little pity party, he hadn't heard the car slow and enter the parking lot.

He tried to wipe away his tears before he turned and saw Bette standing at the edge of the rock.

"Dane? What are you doing out here by yourself?" she asked.

With a sniff he replied, "I needed to be alone. They keep whispering about me."

"Oh, honey, come here. Let's go over to the house and get you warm, you must be freezing." She held out her hand. "Does Cassie know you're out here by yourself?"

He shuffled to her, head down in defeat. "No. I didn't think…"

"Hey, it's okay. We'll call her and let her know you're safe and with me." She held out her hand. "Come on, I'm sure we've got some hot chocolate mix in the cupboard. Doesn't that sound good?"

He put his hand in hers and let her guide him to her car.

"Let me get your bike, it should fit in the trunk."

He slumped in the seat and rubbed at the tears on his face. When had he turned into such a crybaby?

Bette got in the car and looked at him. "It'll be okay, Dane."

She drove them the mile to Mark's house and pulled in next to his car. He shuffled after her, slowly climbing the porch steps after she opened the door.

"Come on in, Dane. Hang your coat on the hook," she said as she went across the kitchen to the fridge. "First, let's get warmed up." She busied herself making the hot chocolate as Dane parked himself on one of the barstools. Once things were in motion, she called Cassie to explain that Dane was with her but left out the part that she'd found him alone at the quarry.

He was surprised. "Why didn't you tell her the truth?" he asked as she placed a mug of hot chocolate in front of him, along with a plate of cookies.

"I didn't lie to her; I just didn't tell her everything." She blew on her mug to cool the steaming cocoa. "It would only make her worry more than she already was. She was just about ready to call Logan to start looking for you."

Tracing a pattern on the countertop, he looked up at her. "Am I in trouble?"

"Not this time, but this can't happen again." She took a bite of cookie and chewed. Mark walked into the room, stopping to give her a kiss.

"Hi, Dane." He grabbed a cookie. "Oooh, I didn't know you baked."

With a laugh she answered, "Yeah. And I clean, too."

"I think I got the better end of this deal." He grabbed another cookie on his way out of the room. "I better get back to my painting."

Dane looked at her with wide eyes. "Are you living here?"

She came around the island and sat next to him. "Yes, so you can come see me if you need to talk. But you've got to promise me one thing—you have to tell Cassie or Logan where you are. If you don't, you'll be in trouble with me; and probably with Cassie, too."

"Okay, I promise." He ate another cookie and drained his mug. "Sometimes, I can't block out all the whispers and I have to get away."

"You are always welcome here, but you need to call first and make sure I'm home."

He nodded. "Okay."

"Now, let's talk about these whispers."

"I know what my dad did was wrong, but Cassie explained that he was sick and needed help."

"Yes, and she's right about both. People don't understand that mental illness is just like any other illness. It's not something that can be wished away."

"Cassie said my dad is in a special prison for people that have problems like his."

"That's right. They're working to make him well again." She took his mug and rinsed it out before placing it in the dishwasher, along with the empty cookie plate.

He continued to trace the pattern on the countertop with his finger. "I've been thinking about this a lot. Cassie mentioned that someday they may be able to adopt me. I don't want them to."

She turned to face him. "Why not?"

"What if my dad gets better? I mean, maybe I'll be able to go home someday."

Bette watched his face. "Maybe. But it will depend on what the judge says at his trial."

He hopped off the stool. "I don't want him to go to prison. What about me?"

"I'm sure you've got a home with Cassie and Logan as long as you need one. They wouldn't take that away from you."

"But what if I have to leave? How will I get along without Vi?" He covered his mouth with his hands in horror, he hadn't meant to say that out loud. "I didn't mean to say…"

"It's okay," she pulled him into a hug. "Obviously, you love Violet. Whatever happens, that will never change." She brushed the hair out of his eyes. "Now, how about I give you a quick haircut before I take you home? I'm pretty good at it, I used to cut my brother's hair all the time."

Twenty minutes later, they were back in Bette's car and headed across town to Cassie and Logan's. When they pulled up in front of the house, Cassie came running out, practically pulling Dane out of the car. "I was so worried when you didn't get home at the normal time."

Bette winked at him. "See, I told you."

He winked back and got out of the car, stretching to try and work the kinks out of his neck.

He chuckled at the memory, lacing his fingers and stretching his arms over his head. Stress always seemed to settle in the muscles in his neck and shoulders. A breeze blew leaves across the expanse of brown grass, reminding him that winter would be showing its face soon.

He'd gotten to the steps when the front door to the house opened. "Come on in, Dane. I just baked an apple pie."

At the mention of pie, his stomach growled. "I guess skipping lunch wasn't such a good idea."

Bette Fairfield, wife of a descendent of the town founder and self-proclaimed witch, motioned him back into the kitchen. The smell of fresh coffee and warm apples made his stomach rumble again. "Oh my, don't they feed you?" Bette asked with a grin.

"I was busy and skipped lunch."

"Well, give me five minutes and I'll make you a sandwich. Ham still your favorite?"

"You don't have to…"

"Nonsense. You know I'm used to hungry boys. I've always got stuff for sandwiches." She dug around in the fridge while he poured himself a mug of coffee.

She plunked everything in her hands down on the counter and pulled out a plate. He watched as she built a sandwich with ham, swiss, pickles, and mayo. They'd spent many afternoons just like this, her fixing him a sandwich while he watched and an open book in front of him.

"Well, I know you don't need any help with your homework," she quipped.

"I wish. Those days were so much… simpler."

"You're here about the spell book, right?" She sliced the sandwich diagonally and pushed the plate in front of him. "Eat up and then you can have pie." She turned to the stove and picked up a pair of oven mitts. She opened the oven door, and the smell of apples and cinnamon wafted his way.

"I didn't come here for you to feed me."

She turned back and looked at him, her hands on her hips. "I've been feeding you since you were a skinny seven-year-old. I'm not going to stop just because you're a grown man."

He was grateful for their relationship. Whenever he'd felt like he didn't belong, he'd hike out here and spend an afternoon with her. He loved Cassie and Logan and was more than grateful for the home they'd welcomed him into, but there was something really special about this woman. Maybe it was the magic you could practically see rolling off her in waves.

"Eat your sandwich. I've got clothes in the dryer, and then we'll talk about the book."

He picked up the sandwich and took a bite, loving how she could get the perfect combination of flavors. Salty ham, the bite of the swiss cheese, the tartness of the pickle, and the mellowness of the mayo. Perfection. He chewed thoughtfully, letting his mind go blank to enjoy the simple act of eating for the first time since Vi had been taken.

Brushing the crumbs off his hands, he turned when he heard the front door open and close, a cool breeze sweeping through the kitchen.

"Dane, I thought that was your car." Dr. Mark Fairfield, Bette's husband, remarked as two identical teenage boys trooped in after him, dropping backpacks to the floor.

"Oooh, apple pie!" Billy exclaimed as MJ picked up an apple from the bowl on the counter and took a bite.

"Homework first; basketball later?"

"Sure, Dad," they said in unison as they grabbed their backpacks and retreated to their room.

Mark sat next to Dane at the bar. "Apple pie? That woman is trying to make me fat."

Dane laughed because Mark was anything but fat. Between their two boys and his job at the hospital, he kept active.

Dane remembered the trouble they'd had when their relationship was new. Dr. Mark had happened upon the accident that brought them both to Fairfield Corners. Locked in the back of their camper truck, Bette had been injured in the crash. His father had kidnapped Bette, believing she'd be the perfect mother for his son. He'd spent five years in prison for that crime, finally getting the psychological help he'd needed. He shoved the thoughts of his father to the back of his mind to be dealt with later. When he was about ten, he'd asked Bette if she'd have dated his dad if he'd asked instead of kidnapping her.

"Probably, but then something else would have brought us here. We were fated to be here."

He knitted his brows. "You really believe that?"

"How can you live in this town with everything we've gone through and *not* believe it?" She sliced into the pie and scooped out a perfect piece. Turning to the fridge, she pulled out a tub of whipped topping, scooping out a huge blob and plopping it on the slice.

She giggled, "Just how you like it—a little pie with your whipped cream."

"Thank you." He knew from experience that a heartfelt thank you went a long way with her. "Don't tell Cassie, but your pies are the best."

Mark and Bette both laughed. "Your secret is safe with us," Beth said as she covered the rest of the pie. She grinned at Mark's sad puppy-dog eyes. "*You* have to wait until after dinner."

"Worth a shot," Mark shrugged with a grin, grabbing an apple from the bowl. Dane was struck by his resemblance to the boys. Without the gray at his temples, he could almost have passed as an older brother. "I'll give you two some privacy to talk about witchy stuff." He walked out of the kitchen toward the den on the other side of the house.

"Finish your pie. I'll go get the book." She turned and hurried out of the kitchen to what Mark and the boys called her witchy room. She returned with the volume in her arms.

He got up, picked up his plates and silverware, and put them in the dishwasher, refilling his coffee on the way back to his seat. "I sure hope you got something useful out of that, we're at dead-ends all over the place."

"Well, to start with, judging by the ink and paper, this was written sometime in the late 1700s.

"That old? Wow."

"In order to summon the demon permanently, the spell needs to be cast on Halloween."

He thought about that for a moment. "That's in a couple of weeks." His face paled as he shot to his feet, the food he'd consumed swirling in his stomach.

"When we found Vi, it looked like Caleb had been performing a spell. He might have killed her if he was doing the possession spell."

"Vi is to be the new host?" she asked.

"I think so. I've got to go…"

"One more thing, Dane. With magic this powerful, stopping a spell after it's started could have serious consequences."

"Well shit." He picked up his keys, walked over to her, and gave her a hug. "Thanks for the info. I've got to let James and Logan know we have to find this mother fucker before he can try again."

Chapter Seventeen

VIOLET

Violet's body trembled as she puked again. *Seriously, what the hell?* Even the thought of food the last couple of days had her running to the bathroom. No fever or other symptoms, just incessant nausea. Her brain finally kicked in and she realized what was going on. Could she be pregnant? She thought back, and it dawned on her. They'd given her antibiotics when her rope burns had started to become infected.

She sat on the floor in front of the toilet with a silly grin on her face. A baby boy with Dane's dark hair and her blue eyes. Lost in thought, she got up and flushed, rinsing her mouth to get rid of the vomit taste. First order of business was a pregnancy test.

The door rattled. "Violet, honey, you okay?"

"Yeah, Mom. I'll be out in a sec."

Her mom stood outside the door, a can of ginger ale in her hand. "This will help. Small sips."

She hugged her. This woman had always been there for her.

"Ragan came in a few minutes ago with a bag for you from the drugstore."

She rolled her eyes. "I wanted Dane to be the first to know. Oh, geez. I suppose everyone knows, now." She opened the soda and sipped at it, hoping it would settle her stomach.

"Yeah, well, secrets are hard to keep in Fairfield Corners."

She followed her mother out to the sales floor, sticking her tongue out at her Aunt Ragan. "You just had to, didn't you," she griped.

Ragan shrugged. "I didn't think...but sorry, not sorry."

Setting the can on the counter she hugged her. "It's okay. But no telling anyone else until I get a chance to tell Dane. He should have been the first to know." She picked up the can and took another sip. "Now, go make sure Mom doesn't tell everyone who walks in the door. Please?"

"Okay. I've got your back, Violet."

The tinkling of the bell signaled another customer. She whispered, "Go. *Hurry*, before she tells..." she looked over and saw Dane in the doorway, waiting for his eyes to adjust to the dimmer lighting inside the store. "...never mind."

She hurried over to Dane. "Hey, big guy. We need to talk." She grabbed his hand and dragged him to the office before someone could let something slip.

She pointed to a chair. "Sit down."

"I need a kiss first," he growled before he pulled her close and kissed her until she was lucky to remember her own name.

"I really need to thank whoever taught you to kiss like that," she mumbled. *Oh, yeah, the test.* "I need to tell you something."

He brushed the hair off her forehead. "What is it Vi? Is something wrong?" His eyes searched her face.

"No, nothing's wrong. The last few days I've been feeling kind of...off, and I've been sick a couple of times."

"Are you sick? Sit down, let me get you some tea or something..."

"Stop. Sit." She pushed him backward until his legs hit the chair. "I said sit."

"Grouchy much?" he grumbled as he sat and looked up at her.

She got closer and stood in between his legs and bent over to whisper in his ear, "I might be pregnant. I have a test, and I need to take it. Can you sit here until I'm done?"

He gulped. "Okay."

She returned to the bathroom, pulled out the test, and followed the instructions, setting the timer on her phone. Hiding the stick in her sleeve she returned to the office.

"Well?" He asked looking at her expectantly.

"It takes a couple of minutes."

He pulled her down into his lap. Arms around her he asked, "You happy about this? We haven't gotten around to talking about having kids."

"Yes, I am. More than anything."

At that he kissed her again, long and slow until the alarm on her phone dinged.

"Well, let's see." She glanced at the test, and then squinted to be sure there were really two lines. She turned the test around and showed him.

"What does that mean, Vi? Two lines."

"That means you're going to be a daddy!"

"Woohoo!" he yelled as he picked her up and swung her around. "A baby!"

"Well that put you in a better mood," she noted. "What had you looking all scowly? Your music was all black and swirly."

His grumpy face returned.

"What's wrong?" Now she was starting to worry? "Is it Dad?"

"No, nothing like that. Just something to do with Caleb. It can wait until tomorrow. Today, we celebrate!"

She watched as he smiled, but it didn't quite reach his eyes. Something was definitely bothering him.

Dane

A baby. He wanted nothing more from this life than to start a family with Vi, and he didn't care how many kids she wanted. But why now?

He'd left Vi with her mom at the bookstore to go buy some saltine crackers that Cassie assured him would help with the morning sickness. He'd also told Vi he'd get dinner started up in his apartment and to come up when she was ready. Sitting in his car out of the cold wind, he pulled out his phone to text Bette a question.

Dane: I have a question about the spells.

Bette: Fire away.

Dane: What if the host is pregnant? Would the demon possess the mom or the baby?

Bette: Violet's pregnant?

Dane: She just told me 10 min ago

Bette: Not sure. I'll ask the coven.

Dane. Thanks.

Bette: Don't worry, we've got this.

Well, that wasn't reassuring—at all. He drove out to the grocery store and decided to pick up the ingredients to make homemade pizza. Wandering the aisles, he didn't notice Caleb trailing behind him.

The lights were off in the store when he got back, and Vi's car was still in the lot. Grabbing the bag of groceries, he hurried up the stairs, not wanting to be away from his girl for another minute.

He unlocked the door and paused to secure the lock before taking the bag over to the kitchen counter. Looking around, he spied Vi asleep in his bed. The sight of her curled around his pillow knocked him breathless. *God, what did I do to deserve her?* The son of a convicted kidnapper had this beautiful woman in his life and they were starting a family. He really needed to talk to her about getting married. He'd been trying to work up the courage to ask her, so fate had given him a kick in the ass.

He'd put off asking her because it felt so fast. It had only been about eight weeks since they'd gotten over the past hurts and misunderstandings. When she disappeared again, he'd thought he'd lost her forever. Shoving the bag in the fridge, he ran to the bathroom and turned on the shower, stepping in before the water had even turned lukewarm. The water started to warm, pelting his back as he leaned against the wall. All the emotion he'd been holding in for the last few weeks poured out of him in waves of tears, overwhelmed with the love for Vi, his baby, and the terror he'd felt when she'd disappeared. *Oh, for fuck's sake. I was an Army MP. Suck it up, McWilliams.* But once

fingers. It looked like a vine with small leaves twisted through it. "I…" He cleared his throat and started again. "Violet Miller, I've loved you since you were four and I was seven. I'm going to love you forever. Will you marry me?"

"Oh, Dane!" she cried. He could see when she realized it was her ring. "Is that…?"

"Yeah, now I'm kinda glad I never gave it back to you before I left."

She took the ring and looked at from all angles. "I can't even tell where you fixed it."

"It took me weeks to figure out how to do it." He watched her again. "Well? Will you?"

"What?" she looked at him in surprise. "Oh, right. Yes. A thousand times, yes."

He leaned forward and kissed her.

Violet

Dane had fallen asleep with her head in his lap as they watched a movie. The lights were low, but she could see the light glinting on the ring on her left-hand ring finger. She knew he was going to ask her to marry him, but was surprised when he pulled out the ring he'd gotten out of a gumball machine when she was ten. She'd never taken the ring off until it had worn through and snapped. It felt right that it was back on her finger.

So many years spent apart, and all because he'd been scared to tell her he was leaving. Dane had promised her father he would let her grow up and discover herself.

She felt Dane's fingers twining through her hair. Rolling onto her back, she looked up at him. "I thought you were asleep."

"Woke up and discovered my dream came true—you're here and wearing my ring again." He rubbed at the ring. "I can get you a diff…"

"No way," she interrupted, "don't you dare." She kissed the back of his hand as she held it between hers. This ring is ours, and it's perfect."

She sat up and he stood, stretching, being sure Vi was watching as his shirt rode up exposing his abs.

"Show off," she said with a smile. Then she reached over and tickled him.

He grunted and curled up, trying to get away from her fingers. "Stop…shit…no fair!"

Her fingers stilled and dug into his sides as she pulled herself closer to him and stood on tiptoe to press her lips to his, her tongue darting out to taste him.

Hands on her behind, he lifted her so her eyes were level with his, then let her slide down the front of him.

Her eyes drooped as she looked up at him.

"You need sleep." He picked her up and carried her to the bed. "Did you call and make an appointment with the doc?"

"Yeah," she said sleepily as he tucked the blanket around her. "You gonna move in with me or what?" She was waiting for his answer when she dropped off to sleep.

Violet sat up and yawned, wondering where Dane had gotten to. The bathroom door was open, so he wasn't in there. Stretching, she padded over to the bar and found a note:

Vi,

I've got an early shift. Call me when you're ready to go to your appointment. Your dad is practically forcing me to go with you. No really, I want to be there for every appointment even if it's just to have blood drawn.

Your mom made me promise you'd only have one cup of coffee since caffeine is bad for the baby. Don't want Baby Mac hyped up on caffeine.

And yes, I'll move in with you.

Love you forever,

Your Dane

She smiled and pressed the note against her chest. She needed to take a shower before her appointment at eleven. Reaching for her phone, she texted the time to Dane so he could pick her up.

The doctor verified it; she was officially pregnant. She practically skipped through the house as she made room for Dane's things. How in the world were they going to fit his stuff in this little house? She was deep into her closet, strewing her clothes across the room as she decided what needed to be boxed up for storage.

"Vi, honey, where are you?"

She poked her head out of the closet to find Dane standing in the doorway staring at the mess.

"What are you doing?"

"Making room for your clothes."

He laughed. "You don't have to do that."

"Well, yes, I do. If you're moving in, you need space for…"

"I found us a bigger place."

She stood in front of him, her hands on her hips. "We only got engaged last night, so how did you manage to find a place today?"

He laughed. "You know, you're cute when you're trying to look fierce." He picked her up and sat on the bed with her in her lap. "The Anderson's put their house up for sale today. I made us an appointment to look at it in about an hour."

"Oh my, you know I've always loved that house. It needs some love but it's a gorgeous old home."

"Exactly. Now, let me help you put all this away so we can go look at our future home."

She threw everything back into the closet, stopping to kiss her fiancé every couple of trips. By the time they left, she was feeling a little flustered from all the kissing.

Chapter Eighteen

DANE

The last piece of furniture was in its new home. Once they'd made the offer, they were in the house within thirty days as the Anderson's already had a place down in Tennessee near their grandchildren. Now, it was theirs. Vi had teared up when he placed the framed picture of his first Christmas with them on the mantel. He wondered how she would react if he told her about the copy in his photo album, the one with the torn off corners from being taped up near his bunk wherever he was stationed. Showing her that one would have to wait for another day.

After measuring every window, Vi and Cassie, along with Ragan and Faith, were on a mission to find the perfect curtains for each room. This kept them out of the way while the guys moved in the furniture. They still had some rooms to fill but they had bedroom furniture and the living room was livable. The rest they could buy when they had time.

Finally, the house was quiet. The guys had left ten minutes before, and he had the place to himself. Grabbing a beer from the fridge, he strolled through the downstairs and imagined what it would look like fully furnished and kids running around. He mentally shook himself. He needed to see this one born first before worrying about more.

A frisson of fear raced through him, the memory of what happened to his dad when his mom died stopped him in his tracks halfway up the stairs. For years, he'd worried that it was something hereditary and he'd end up doing something just as crazy as kidnapping a stranger. He focused on the coolness of the bottle in his hand to ground him in the present, and he yelled, "That won't happen to me! I have family here." His knees shook; the thought of losing his Vi made him want to puke. *Jesus, I need to get this shit under control.* Impending fatherhood was screwing with his emotions. Once that errant thought was locked back up in his mind, he continued up the stairs.

Imagining a girl that looked like Vi sliding down the banister while a dark-haired boy egged her on made him smile as he ran his hand up the banister. The house echoed with memories yet to be made, and he wanted to add a couple of dogs to his growing family. Logan and Cassie always had at least two dogs running around, if not more, depending on how many needed fostering. Their house was always open to strays whether animal or human. So much love. He sent up a thank you to whatever deity was listening that he'd landed in Fairfield Corners.

The bed which had seemed small in his loft apartment now took up a good portion of the master bedroom. Cassie had set the sheets out so they could make the bed when they returned. He was perfectly capable of making a bed, so he set down his beer and unfolded the sheets. He'd bent over to put the fitted sheet down first when he felt exploding pain and then nothing.

Violet

She was exhausted but they'd found curtains for the windows, and her mom and Marie would be back the next day to help her hang them, but she was sure Dane wouldn't let her climb the ladder to do it.

Rufus whined and tugged at his leash when she opened the door. Since they were home, she let go and let him go investigate whatever had him worked up. She watched him trot up the stairs as she took off her jacket.

"Aroooo," she heard Rufus howl.

"What's wrong, buddy?" she asked as she climbed the stairs. *Maybe a squirrel got in or something.*

She followed the sounds of his howls to the master bedroom, her eyes going to the spreading pool of blood. "What the…" she murmured as she walked around the end of the bed.

Dane was lying face down, Rufus was licking his face and then howling again. Dane wasn't moving.

She dropped to her knees and felt for a pulse, panicking when she couldn't feel one. "No, no, no…"

Dane groaned and she remembered to breathe. *Shit, I have to get help.* With shaking hands, she unlocked her phone and it rang in her hand.

"Daddy? I need help, Dane's hurt and not moving and I…"

"I'm coming, Baby Girl."

Rufus howled again and she dropped her phone into the pool of blood. She picked it up and tried to wipe off the sticky red. *Why won't it come off?*

Footsteps pounded up the steps as Rufus howled again.

Logan ran into the room, phone at his ear as he relayed information to the dispatcher. "Tell that ambulance to hurry, we've got an officer down." Repeating the address again, he pulled Violet to him, put the phone on speaker, and then set it down on the floor.

He saw the blood pooling under Dane's arm. Trying to keep the crime scene intact, he knelt next to him and moved his arm to reveal the gaping slash that went from wrist to elbow. He swallowed hard and tore off his tee shirt, pressing it firmly against the cut to staunch the bleeding and hold the edges of the wound together.

Vi watched, unable to move, trying to comprehend what she was seeing. Who would want to hurt her Dane? And so violently?

"Violet, honey, go put Rufus in his crate."

She looked at him, blinking.

He told her again, this time in his 'I'm your father and you will obey me' voice, "Vivi, go put the dog in his crate. The ambulance will be here soon, and I don't want him to get in the way."

"Oh, okay," she whispered and called to the dog. "Come on, Rufus, baby. Time to kennel up." He started to follow her out of the room but stopped and looked back at Dane and Logan.

"It's okay Rufus, I'll take care of your dad," Logan said before turning his attention back to Dane. "Jesus, that's a lot of blood," he muttered.'

∼

Violet

Rufus walked calmly into his crate and sat, whining. She ruffled his fur and then latched the door. "He'll be okay, baby, he just has to be."

The fog in her mind began to lift, and the sight of Dane lying in a spreading pool of blood was practically tattooed on the back of her eyelids. It was all she saw when she closed her eyes.

A screaming siren and the sounds of yelling came in through the open door. Two EMTs hurried in with a gurney piled with medical supplies.

"Upstairs, first door on the right," she said calmly. Her legs refused support her any longer and she dropped to her knees, her head spinning.

Dane

He opened his eyes and immediately regretted it. The bright light felt like it was piercing his brain.

"Dane? Honey?"

Violet's voice. She sounded exhausted.

He tried opening his eyes again, slowly. The pain was less but still there.

And his arm. It felt heavy and not quite attached to the rest of him.

Cool fingers brushed at his face, and he smiled.

"There you are. God, you scared me." She gripped his hand. He felt that, so that was good… right?

"What happened," he asked and tried to sit up. Pain behind his eyes made him nauseated. He closed his eyes and swallowed hard, willing the bile back down where it belonged. "Remind me not to do that again," he mumbled.

The fogginess parted and he realized he was in a hospital. "Shit, Vi, what happened?"

Mark came in and checked his pupils, the light bringing back the stabbing pain. "Jesus, Doc."

Vi brushed at a tear on her cheek. "Do you remember what happened?"

"I was making the bed." He grinned at the face she made. "I do know how to make a bed, you know. Then it felt like the back of my head exploded." He reached up and felt the bandages on the back of his head.

Mark looked at the chart in his hand. "No skull fracture, thankfully; but you did get fifteen stitches in the back of your head, plus another forty in your arm."

"Jesus," he muttered. "No wonder I feel like I got hit by a truck."

"It's a good thing I got home when I did or…" her eyes filled with tears, and she hung her head. "I'm sorry," she cried and ran out of the room.

He looked at Doc. "Was it really that close?"

"Well, we had to give you a transfusion because you lost a lot of blood. Any longer and it could have been a much worse outcome."

Dane rubbed his forehead with his good hand, wires and tubes trailing. "Can I get something for this headache?"

"Yes, we can do that now that you're awake. I'll get that ordered right now." He walked toward the door. "I'll call Bette and let her know you're awake. She's been helping Cassie deal with getting the bedroom cleaned."

The door snicked closed. He leaned back, closing his eyes and trying to will the pain away.

He must have slept because he woke to find Vi curled up in the chair next to the bed. Her face was too pale. He reached over and brushed the hair away from her face, the bluish bags under her eyes made him wonder how long he'd been here.

The door opened and Bette peeked in. "Good, she's finally sleeping. I'm sure that's not very comfortable but I don't want to wake her."

"How long have I been here? She looks like she hasn't slept in a week."

Bette brushed the hair off his forehead and placed a light kiss there. "They brought you in yesterday afternoon. It was scary for a while, but you responded well to the transfusions."

"More than one? Jesus."

"And don't worry, we made sure Violet ate. We just couldn't get her to sleep. She was so worried about you."

Violet raised her head and looked around. "What time is it?"

Bette took her hand. "Almost five. Do you want me to go get you something to eat down in the cafeteria?"

"That would be nice," Vi nodded as the nurse walked in and checked the IV line and bag.

Dane looked at Vi as she blinked sleepily at him. "You should go home and get some real sleep, Vi."

"No, I'm not ready to do that yet."

There was a knock on the door and Logan walked in. "Cassie told me you were awake."

"Your dad's here, so go with Bette and get something to eat. Please? For me?"

She placed her hand on the side of his face and leaned in to kiss him. Her lips on his got a reaction out of his dick and he groaned. "God, Vi, I can't hardly move, and one kiss has me…" he looked over and saw Logan trying not to laugh. "Just go eat, okay?"

"Okay, Dane." She let Bette lead her out of the room.

Dane sagged, pain clouding his eyes. "Shit, she looks so lost."

"Hey, she's just worried about you. Plus, all those pregnancy hormones can't be helping. Bette will make sure she eats."

"Tell me you know who did this." Dane's eyes flared with anger.

"Yes, we got some usable prints off the windowsill where he gained entry through a broken window."

Dane watched Logan's face. "It was her ex, wasn't it? Dammit, I…"

Logan put his hand on Dane's shoulder.

"Calm down. You rip out all those stitches and Doc will have my hide."

Dane blew out a long breath and tried to calm himself. "What are you doing to find him?"

"We've got an APB out on him and a description of his car. The State Police have been brought in. He's not going to get away."

"You've got to keep Vi safe. I don't know what I'd do if anything happened to her."

"There's a statie outside your house and another in front of the bookstore. We'll keep her safe."

"What about The Pub?" I'm sure she's going to want to start singing again."

"We'll deal with that when it happens. Adam told her she could take off as much time as she needed. She's always had him wrapped around her little finger."

Dane yawned, wincing at the pain it caused in his head.

Logan put a hand on Dane's shoulder. "You need to sleep; best way to heal."

"Feels like I've been sleeping for a week already."

Logan huffed a laugh. "I remember that feeling. Let Violet pamper you a little. You know, you had us all scared, but Vi wouldn't hardly leave your side to let the doctors treat you."

Dane's eyes drifted shut. "Love her more than life itself."

Logan leaned back in the chair and closed his eyes.

Violet

"Daddy, you're supposed to be watching him, not taking a nap."

Logan blinked, "Huh?"

"Hey Vi," Dane said from the bed, dragging her attention away from her father. "Give him a break, it's been a rough couple of days."

Logan stood and stretched. "I better get back to the house, I'm sure your mother will be stopping by this evening."

She ran over and hugged him. "Love you, Daddy."

"Love you too, Vivi." He looked over at Dane. "Make sure she gets some sleep."

Dane grinned, "I'll do what I can, but you know she's her own woman."

Logan rolled his eyes. "Yeah, just like her mother."

Once he was gone Vi took her usual place in the chair next to the bed. "You look like you feel a little better."

Chapter Nineteen

VIOLET

Dane had fallen asleep on the couch while watching a football game, Rufus curled up beside him. She tiptoed out of the house, thanking God again that he was okay. All this trouble because she picked a fiancé with ulterior motives. *See?* she told herself, *I should have taken a peek at his music.* Now that she knew what an asshole he was, she was curious as to what his song looked like.

The manhunt for Caleb was ongoing and she knew sneaking out wasn't the smartest move, but she needed some time to herself. This time of year, the Island would be deserted so that's where she was headed. A fire would keep her warm and then she could think without some hulking man intruding. Surely, Caleb had hightailed it out of the state after attacking Dane. Was it in retaliation for her breaking off the engagement or was it something more sinister?

She was almost to the lake when her phone started blowing up with text notifications and then ringing. Shit, Dane must be awake. She parked in the clearing near the shoreline and frowned at her phone.

Her fingers flew across the keyboard.

I'm at the Island – needed time away to think. I'll call you in an hour. DO NOT send anyone after me.

She hit send and turned off her ringer, setting an alarm for an hour so she didn't lose track of the time.

So much had happened in the ten months since she returned to Fairfield Corners. Absently rubbing her stomach, she vowed to protect the child growing there. No noticeable baby bump yet, but there would be soon. They'd nicknamed him or her Baby Mac, and the child would be loved and protected. She let herself imagine a time after their current troubles were in the past, heaping love on this baby and her family.

After gathering some kindling and small branches, she used the lighter from her pocket to start a fire, holding hands near the flames to warm them. Lost in thought, she didn't hear the shuffling behind her.

"Did you really think I would go away that easily?" she heard whispered in her ear.

Her lungs stilled and her heart thundered. *Shit, why did I come out here alone?* It had seemed like such a good idea at the time.

He dragged her to her feet and toward his car, which was now tan instead of blue. Probably had a stolen license plate on it to stay off the cops' radar.

"I don't want any trouble from you. Will you sit still and behave, or do I need to tie you up?" He laughed, "Oh yeah, forgot who I was talking to." He opened the trunk and pulled out some zip ties, using one to tie her hands together behind her back.

She held her lips together, trying not to let them tremble. No way would she show this asshat how terrified she was.

He pulled her phone out of her coat pocket and tapped on the screen and smiled. "So predictable." Caleb tsked. "You never changed your pin."

Crap, I should have changed that…

"Let's see how much Mr. Hotshot Policeman loves his woman and baby."

She watched as he selected a number and held her breath, knowing he was calling Dane. *Dammit.*

He held the phone toward her, "Tell him to meet you here. And no funny stuff."

"Vi? Dammit, why did you leave? And why the Island?"

"I wanted to spend some time out here with you. Come meet me, I've got a nice fire going." She hoped he got the message since she'd already texted him that she wanted time alone.

"I'll be there in a few. Love you, Violet."

She hoped him calling her Violet instead of Vi meant he understood. Looking down at her feet she prayed he would come with the sheriff's department to back him up.

Caleb tossed her phone to the ground and then shoved her into the car. Taking a folded paper out of his pocket he unfolded it, and his smile turned her blood cold. "This should bring him running." From another pocket he pulled a folded hunting knife. Unfolding it he speared the paper, pinning it to the log she'd been sitting on.

"Dammit Caleb, why are you doing this?"

"I've given up on you being the vessel. I found a better one."

"Then what do you need me and Dane for?" Her eyes widened as a thought crept into her brain. "No. You cannot have my baby. I will die before I let you use my child."

"That can be arranged. You're what, eight weeks along?" He smiled again as he put the car in drive and took off. "Yeah, I've been watching you, living your happy little life. A dog, a kid, and now a house. Lucky for me."

"Caleb, you can't do this!" she yelled. Remembering how singing had brought forth something the last time she started humming, willing the magic to return and help her.

The car skidded to a stop in the middle of the road. He turned and stared at her, that sick smile on his face. Pulling a rag from the back seat he stuffed it into her mouth and tied it at the back of her head, effectively gagging her. "Can't have that happening again."

Her eyes filled with tears. Her music tried to build but the gag effectively cut her off from that magic. She'd pushed everything that happened that day in the bunker out of her mind, now she wished she'd have tried to cultivate whatever it was that she'd done to thwart his plans. The beat of the song pounded at her temples, making her dizzy. The music needed to be set free, that much she knew. Unable to control it, she watched as his song swirled in black and gray rotten looking streaks around the car. She'd never seen anyone's song look like that, like the song itself was rotten.

She was losing track of time as the music pounded in her head, blocking out reality. All of her energy was spent trying to keep from being sick. She didn't know if it was the music or the baby, but she did know she would probably choke if she puked while gagged.

Suddenly, they stopped and Caleb pulled her from the car. Her legs didn't get the message and she fell to her knees in the dirt. She recognized the place, and the music changed pitch because it did, too. The yellow crime scene tape flapped from the doorframe of the bunker.

Shit. I hope Dane and Dad think to check here.

A vice-like grip on her arm, Caleb pulled her down the stairs and threw her onto a chair. As her eyes adjusted to the flickering light from a fire, she could make out a bowl of dark liquid on a table, along with a knife and some twine-wrapped packets. With a laugh, Caleb sauntered over to the table and opened a packet. "Some of your hair," he said as he dropped it into the bowl. "And some of his." He stirred the concoction and then turned back to her.

"Now, I just need a little of your blood. Already got quite a bit of your policeman's."

Her head swam. *That's why he attacked Dane, he needed his blood.* She worked at the gag, trying to push it out of her mouth. She had to be able to sing.

Drawing the knife down her arm to make a small cut, he watched blood dribble into a bowl. "It was much more satisfying to watch the blood pump out of the long gash on your man's arm. So rich and red, like a river." He took the bowl, mumbled something over it, and then poured it into the bowl of Dane's blood.

Maybe if she hummed, the magic would come. Her mind went blank, and then remembered it was Ragan's Song she'd sung when the magic had come to help. Humming the melody, she continued to work on the gag, and it began to loosen.

Finally able to push the gag out of her mouth with her tongue, she tried to sing but all that came out was a croak. Her mouth and throat were so dry, she had to wait for her saliva to moisten them enough to sing out some true notes.

She croaked out a few notes and stopped again, watching as swirls of magic appeared above the bowl of blood he was stirring. Just thinking about how much blood was in that bowl made her stomach roll. Dane had almost died so this asshat could do his little magic spell.

"You know why I needed so much blood? The demon requires it, and it eases the demon's installation into the host. I couldn't risk taking that much blood from you, the baby must be protected as the host. When his blood mingles with yours in the bowl, the master can then begin the transformation."

The swirls collided and morphed into a globe and started spinning. Neon green eyes within the globe opened and Caleb laughed as he danced around the room. "It's working! I knew I had that spell memorized. Helagong is rising again—he'll be reborn in this child." He returned to the table and chanted aloud as he raised his hands in supplication.

I can't let him do this, I must protect my baby. She tried to sing again, and a few notes rang true before her voice cracked.

The door beside her creaked open, the sound lost in Caleb's chanting. Dane stood in the doorway, his eyes dark, almost black in anger.

"Dane," she whispered. "Help me,"

Either Dane didn't hear her or he ignored her. He strode forward, gun in hand, as he closed the distance between him and Caleb.

Caleb flicked his hand and Dane's gun went flying across the room. "No need for that." Another flick and Dane flew across the room and was pinned to the wall, his feet a foot off the floor. He struggled, but he was pinned like a butterfly in a collection.

It was up to her to save all three of them. Sending up a prayer she opened her mouth and prepared to let her strongest note fly.

"I wouldn't if I were you," Caleb said with a smirk. "I remember what happened the last time I let you sing down here." He made a complex move with his hand and it was if the gag was back. No matter what she tried she was mute.

The globe with the glowing eyes was changing, becoming misty and she could see through it as it swirled.

Caleb chanted louder and the mist wafted toward her, moving faster as it got closer.

Her music hurled itself against whatever he'd thrown up to block it, and she could feel it cracking. Finally, it cracked enough to let her music through.

She took a deep breath, and sang a note so pure it couldn't be duplicated. As if shot out of a cannon, it barreled toward the mist, plowing into it and scattering it to the corners of the room. She had no idea what she needed to sing next. The music poured out of her on a river of magic, its notes finally free and swirling through the air. She finally had her own song, the notes whirling around her in reds and golds as they gathered together and shot toward the misty globe.

The mist disappeared with a pop and Caleb screamed in frustration. "No! He will not be denied again!"

The magic surged and blanketed Caleb, pinning his arms to his sides. The bowl of blood bubbled furiously, streaks of magic churning above it.

What the hell? Then she remembered Bette's warning that the spells from the book were so powerful that stopping before the spell was completed could have dire consequences.

The magic coiled and swelled, ruffling the handwritten pages scattered on the table. Caleb hurried to the book and rifled through the pages, looking for the spell he'd been casting, but the magic ripped the pages from his hands—it was obviously too late.

Caleb's eyes widened as her magic solidified into a form, its arms reaching for him.

"I'm sorry! It isn't my fault. I tried…" and then he was wrapped in magic so tightly he couldn't move. The magic lifted him off the floor and squeezed the life out of him.

Vi watched as his essence, an ugly grayish green color, joined the magic and then dissipated. Caleb dropped to the floor, lifeless.

A wisp of magic wafted to Dane and released him from the wall, gently dropping him to the floor as another released Violet from her bonds and the rest of the magical gag disappeared completely. She dropped to her knees, exhausted.

"Vi, honey, are you okay?" She could feel Dane's arms around her, but she was so tired she couldn't find the energy to move.

"I think so," she whispered, and then she slept.

Dane

He dropped to his knees and checked for a pulse, his heart thundering in his chest. It was there— faint, but there. He wrapped her in his arms and collapsed to the floor.

With a crash, the door at the top of the stairs opened, a crowd of police led by James and Logan poured down the stairs.

Logan dropped to his knees next to Dane, "Is she…"

"She's alive." Dane kissed the top of her head as a tear ran down his face. "She saved us all."

Once it was verified that Caleb was dead, they led Bette down the stairs and into the chamber.

"Please, clear the room. We won't disturb any evidence, but we need to be sure the magic released by the spell went back where it came from." Bette's voice rang with the authority due as the coven leader.

Logan took Violet from Dane's arms, frowning when Dane stumbled. "You both need the hospital. There's an ambulance…"

Dane interrupted, "Don't worry about me. Worry about her and the baby."

Logan rushed up the stairs with Vi in his arms. Dane stumbled behind him, his legs rubbery like he'd run a marathon. He finally made it to the top of the stairs where an EMT helped him onto a gurney.

Logan

The air practically vibrated with magic as they pulled up next to Dane's car. *God, don't let us be too late.* He'd battled this demon once, and he would do it again to save his family.

The whoop of sirens filled the air as state and local police poured into the clearing, James leading the way.

Logan was the first to the door, James right behind him. The door rattled on its hinges but wouldn't open. James yelled over his shoulder for a battering ram, trembling as he waited and praying they weren't too late. He blinked at the searing pain radiating from the small space the demon once used to try and take him over in order to hurt Cassie all those years ago.

Pounding on the door, the pain ebbed and flowed as his daughter and foster son battled the magic intent on raising the green-eyed demon again. His daughter's voice, that beautiful voice, rang out over the din created by the swirling magic. The tune struck a memory deep inside him of an ethereal place of mist and haze that he barely remembered. The place where he'd met a woman important to Cassie who had been dead for months. The woman who'd helped him subdue the demon and send it away—they'd thought that meant forever.

The door blew inward and Logan ran down the steps, his feet barely touching the steps, no thought in his mind except getting to his daughter. Bile rose in his throat when he saw Dane sprawled on the floor, Violet in his lap, tears streaming down his face.

Oh, God, we're too late. The pain he'd felt in his head moved to his heart. Rocks dug into his knees unheeded when he dropped next to Dane. "Is she…?" He couldn't finish the sentence.

"She's alive." His heart squeezed as Dane kissed the top of her head. "She saved us all."

She was alive but she wasn't awake, wasn't moving. He barely heard Bette commanding everyone out of the chamber. He stood and took his Vivi into his arms, allowing Dane to stand. "You both need the hospital, there's an ambulance…"

He frowned when Dane stumbled. He was awake but Violet wasn't.

Dane urged him to go ahead, "Don't worry about me. Worry about her and the baby."

He rushed to the stairs knowing Dane would follow. The scene outside the chamber was controlled chaos, with James trying to direct cops where they were needed. He caught James's eye and James pointed across the clearing to the ambulances. Pushing through the crowd, Vivi lay limp and lifeless in his arms, but he could see the faintest flutter of a pulse in her neck. His lips moved in a silent plea, "Don't let *my* baby die—and don't let *her* baby die."

133

He laid Violet on a gurney and kissed her forehead, taking her cold hand in his. "Hang on Baby Girl," he choked back a sob. "Dane needs you. Losing you would kill him."

As if she'd heard him, Violet sighed.

Tears ran down his face as he bent over her and whispered, "I'll go get Dane."

He turned and found Dane limping toward him, his face drawn and tired. The battle had taken a lot out of him.

The EMT called out, "We're ready to go. You riding along?"

Logan pushed Dane toward the ambulance. "Go get checked out. Take care of our girl; we'll meet you there."

The ambulance left with a whoop of the siren.

Phone in hand, Logan walked to his cruiser—it was time to call Cassie.

Chapter Twenty

CASSIE

"I'm staying with her. You can't make me leave!"

She followed Dane's yelling to where Violet lay on a bed, hooked up to monitors and an IV.

"Dane, honey, I'm here."

He sagged, dropping into a chair. "I can't stand to let her out of my sight."

The tears running down his face squeezed her heart. "They've got to run their tests. They need to find out what's wrong so they can fix it."

"I just..."

Mom mode kicked in and she walked over to him. "Come here," she said, arms wide for a hug.

He stepped into her arms, his hug almost crushing her. And then he went limp.

The nurse stepped closer, grabbing his arm as Cassie staggered under the weight of a six-foot-two, heavily muscled man. They lowered him into the chair and the nurse called for help as she started checking his vitals. The bluish smudges under his eyes had her worried.

They brought in a gurney, got him on it, and prepared to move him to another curtained area for evaluation.

"Can he be close? If he wakes up and he's not near her…"

The nurse checked the next bay. "Curtain four is available. We can open the curtain between them; will that work?"

"Yes, thank you. He's stubborn and would pitch a fit if…"

"Vi?" she heard him murmur.

Cassie took his hand and held it as they moved the gurney to the adjacent area. "Shhh, she's right there. I can see her." Moving out of the way she pointed to Violet in the nearby bed.

"Okay," he mumbled before he started snoring.

Cassie sat between the beds, her attention going from one to the other and back again.

The doctor finished his tests on Violet and turned to Cassie. "We can't find anything wrong with her. She seems to be in a natural sleep. Her blood pressure is a little low, so we've treated that with IV fluids."

"What about the baby?"

"Everything looks normal. My best guess at this point is extreme exhaustion."

Her head snapped up at the deep, "Thank God," coming from her husband.

She jumped up and ran to Logan. "You heard? Both Violet and the baby are fine."

The doctor went over to Dane and conferred with the nurse. "It looks like his condition is the same." He grinned. "The snoring is a good sign." He scrawled some notes on the chart. "We'll get them set up in a regular room for monitoring, probably overnight."

Cassie leaned against Logan and put her arms around him. "Our babies are okay, all three of them."

Dane

The next morning Cassie and Logan returned to the hospital to find Violet curled up in Logan's bed, his arms wrapped around her.

Violet stirred when Cassie brushed the hair off her forehead. "Hey, Mom." She snuggled into Dane.

He groaned, "I told you to stop that, I'm not doing that here." He grunted and laughed when she tickled him. "Brat."

"Mom and Dad are here, behave."

He opened one eye and peered up at Cassie and Logan standing at the end of the bed. They were both smiling, that was a good sign. With a yawn, he sat up and adjusted the bed, pulling Vi closer to him, relieved she was safe in his arms.

Logan pulled a chair closer to the bed for Cassie and then leaned against the wall. "I don't think you two sharing a bed was what the doctor agreed to."

Violet's face flashed red, and she nestled closer to Dane. "I don't care."

Dane looked at Logan. "Is he really dead?"

"Yes, and according to Bette the demon is gone for good this time. They destroyed the pages so there's no chance he'll be resurrected again."

Violet ran her hands through her hair and grimaced. "As much as I love lying here in bed with you, I really need a shower. I feel like his rotten song coated me in that gross gray green."

Cassie stood and picked up one of the bags they'd dropped near the door. "We brought you clothes and stuff. Let's go get you cleaned up."

She dropped her feet to the floor and slid off the bed, being careful to keep the back of the hospital gown closed.

Cassie pulled her close with one arm and they walked over to the bathroom and closed the door.

Dane rubbed his hands over his face, wanting a shower for himself. "It's really over? Gone forever?"

"Bette assures me he is."

"And I can't say I'm sorry that poor excuse for a man is dead. That he used Vi…" The anger vibrated off him and Logan grinned.

"The first time I laid eyes on him, I knew something wasn't right. And when none of the dogs liked him, that clinched it for me."

The bathroom door opened and he looked up to find his Vi dressed in a long, dark-green tunic and some kind of leggings that showed off her figure. He stared, his thoughts going to how much fun it would be to strip those down her legs and…" He swallowed hard and grinned at her. "I hope we get released soon. I want to take you home and…" He stopped at the look on Logan's face. "…uh, make you lunch."

Logan choked back a laugh. "Good save, son." He crossed his arms and glared at Dane. "And since you knocked up my daughter, you better start planning a wedding."

"I would marry her today if she'd agree to it. That being said, I want her to have the wedding of her dreams, no matter how long that takes."

Cassie and Violet looked at each other and giggled. Cassie took Violet's hand and pulled her toward the door. "Let's go see if that doctor will release you both soon."

Once they were out the door, Dane took his own shower.

Violet

When they were far enough away from the room not to be heard, Vi turned to her mom. "I want to marry him today. Can we do a surprise wedding?"

Cassie pulled out her phone. "Let's call Ragan and get the ball rolling. She'll wrangle the troops and get everything set up. Do you have a dress?"

"I do," she said with a laugh. I bought it after our first date—I knew then he was it for me. I saw the dress, and it was perfect."

Cassie spoke into her phone, "Ragan, I need…well, Violet needs your help."

Plans for the wedding in place, and the decorating and reception being handled by Ragan, they tracked down the doctor who signed the release paperwork for them both.

"I think that's everything. I'm ready to go tell Dane he better put his money where his mouth is." She twirled and Cassie laughed.

They returned to the room and Dane was zipping up the bag that had held his change of clothes.

Violet waved the paperwork in her hand. "We're released. You ready to go get married?"

"What?" Dane asked as he turned to look at her.

"I'm taking you up on your offer to marry you today."

Dane grabbed her hand and pulled her up against him. "Are you serious? Don't you want a church, and flowers, and all that shit?"

"No. My perfect wedding is you and me in front of our family and friends. Ragan is getting The Pub ready right now."

Dane picked her up and swung her around. "Woohoo! We're getting married today!" he crowed.

Logan laughed. "We better get you two to the courthouse for a marriage license. Good thing there's no waiting period in Indiana."

He pulled Vi toward the door. "Let's go."

Later that afternoon…

Violet turned from the mirror. "See? Told you it was the perfect dress." Off white, the long skirt brushed the floor. "Do we have everything?"

Cassie ticked off the items, "Something old is your grandmother's ring, something borrowed is Jenna's hair clip, something blue is your garter. Now for something new." She dug around in her purse and pulled out a box. "This is from your dad and me."

Violet removed the lid and gasped. The earrings were long and dangly, something she would have picked out for herself. Gold and diamonds sparkled as she lifted one to her ear. "Oh Mom, they're perfect." She put in one, then the other, and turned to the mirror for a look. "How did you find these on such short notice?"

"We bought these for Christmas a month ago. But I'm so glad to be giving them to you today, for this occasion."

Violet wiped at a tear. "Mom, don't make me cry," she said with a laugh. "I don't want to have to redo my makeup." She tucked a stray curl behind her ear. "Is everything ready?"

The music drifting down the stairs halted when someone unplugged the jukebox in the middle of a song. She strained to hear the melody and gasped when she realized it was the song her Uncle Adam had been working on for his new album. "Oh wow, that is beautiful."

Logan walked into the room. "You look beautiful, Vivi." He kissed her cheek and then held out his arm. "That's our cue. You ready?"

She smiled up at him. "I've been waiting for this day since I was four."

Dane

Standing in front of the stage, Dane nervously watched the doors at the back of the room. *Sure, she said she'd marry me today, but what if she'd changed her mind?*

Ragan, along with Faith and Bette, had transformed The Pub into an intimate space, perfect for a wedding. The tables had been moved to create a central aisle leading up to where Dane waited anxiously.

Adam clapped him on the shoulder. "Don't worry, she's just waiting for her cue. Relax and breathe."

He let out a gush of air and stuck his hands in his pockets. *Why am I so nervous? I've wanted this forever.*

The room hushed when the jukebox cut out in the middle of a song. Everyone turned to the back of the room expectantly when Adam pulled out a guitar and started strumming a hauntingly beautiful melody.

And then she was there in the doorway, on her father's arm. Not much about their wedding was traditional but she was being walked down the aisle by her beloved father.

She looked up and his eyes filled with tears. Her off-white dress swept the floor, with long flowing sleeves and a deep neckline that showed off her beautiful cleavage. He blinked to get that thought out of his head or he'd cut the ceremony short to ravish his bride.

"Deep breath dumb ass," he whispered to himself as she started down the aisle toward him. He saw flashes of impossibly high heels, and he marveled at her ability to walk without falling off them.

His heart thundered as she walked toward him, and he realized he finally felt totally at home. For many years, he'd felt like something was missing. Sure, he had a loving home with Cassie, Logan, and Violet, and whatever other foster kids they had at the time, but this was the first time he'd felt completely at ease. The many years spent wondering if his father's influence during his younger years would materialize and ruin everything were finally behind him. He felt like he'd won the lottery. The most beautiful woman in the world was walking toward him to promise herself to him forever.

Suddenly, Logan was there and placing her hand in his. His heart wanted to explode with joy. She was finally going to be his. "So beautiful," he murmured and then kissed her, long and slow, with every emotion he was feeling. He looked up guiltily when someone cleared their throat.

"Oops, sorry, couldn't help myself."

Everyone laughed and the wedding proceeded, tying together two people whose pasts were inexorably entwined together.

And finally, it was time to kiss her again. They were married, and Dane was a very happy man.

Epilogue

VIOLET

Violet rocked the chair as she looked down at the precious girl in her arms. She'd gotten her wish—Evie had her father's dark hair and it looked like she would have her mama's bright blue eyes. "Well, she's got the eyes…I wonder if she's got the music, too?" she mused as she hummed a lullaby.

A floorboard creaked and she looked up to find her husband standing in the doorway, the most wonderful of surprises in his arms. Evie's twin, DJ, was a total shock. He'd been hiding behind his sister the entire pregnancy, so in tune with his sister that their hearts beat at the same time, helping to keep him a secret.

"He started fussing but seems to have settled down now that he's closer to his sister." Dane carefully sat in the other rocker so he wouldn't disturb the baby in his arms.

"How did we get so lucky? Two beautiful babies."

He smiled and kissed his son on the top of his head, slowly rocking to help the baby sleep.

Violet held out her hand and Dane took it. They sat and rocked, marveling at the love in the room. She watched as the twins' songs reached out and intertwined, pink and blue swirls frolicking above their heads.

Once the babies were both down for the night, Vi kissed Dane and headed for her music studio. It had originally been built as a large shed, but Dane had enlarged it and upgraded it to be usable all year by insulating it and installing a small furnace. She picked up her favorite guitar and headed for the small recording room—a surprise cooked up by her husband and uncle. Now, she could work on solo recordings if she wished. As she ambled to the recording room, she ran her hand along the framed Hot 100 listing that showed her debut song at number one. When she'd come home to Fairfield Corners, she'd thought that her life would be quiet as she worked on her music career. But it seemed fate had other ideas, throwing her back into Dane's life on a lonely stretch of highway. She sent up a silent prayer to whatever deity had a hand in that.

She'd resigned herself to a life with Caleb, a guy she thought she loved. Turned out, he wasn't the one, Dane was. And for that, she was eternally thankful. Somehow, a four-year-old girl knew who she was destined to share her life with.

Taking a seat, she did some final tuning to her guitar and started recording. As she strummed and sang, the lyrics poured out of her in a wave of love—love for Dane, love for her babies, and love for her life.

Meanwhile, Dane went to his workshop in the garage, baby monitor in hand, The space had been aptly christened The Testosterone Zone by his wife. He'd found a new passion to go along with his passion for his life and his family: building custom guitars. His first creation was currently Vi's favorite guitar for songwriting. As he sanded and shaped his newest creation, he checked the specs. This one was for Fletch Carmichael, lead singer of Ground Zero who'd asked about one for himself after seeing Vi's.

What had started as something to keep him busy while Vi worked had turned into a business. Having contacts in the music industry definitely helped. The money would go into college funds for the babies. *How did I get so lucky?*

About the Author

Romance author, dialysis warrior, furkid mom, and Best Fiends addict. Lover of coffee, 80's music, and all things romance. During the day she carves out writing time in between trips to the back door as doorman to her four-legged furry child. At night after spending quality time with her husband she chips away at her never-ending TBR pile.

Keep up with Hoosiergirl Publishing here:
https://hoosiergirl-publishing.kit.com/df28902ff9

You can find all her links on her website:
https://www.laremenicky.com

Also by L.A. REMENICKY

https://www.lavishpublishing.com/authors/l-a-remenicky/

Saving Cassie (Fairfield Corners Book 1) - Everyone has secrets. Sometimes secrets can get you killed. After ten years in the big city, Cassie Holt is moving back to her hometown to take over the bookstore left to her by her beloved Gram, vowing to live her life alone. To her best friend, Sheriff James Marsten, Cassie seems to be the same girl that left Fairfield Corners to go to college but Cassie has secrets and one of those secrets could get her killed. When one of her secrets becomes a threat to her life, James turns to his new deputy to help him keep Cassie safe. Deputy Logan Miller has been burned by love and is not looking to get involved with anyone anytime soon. When he is thrown into close quarters with Cassie, the sparks begin to fly and he begins to see through the walls Cassie has built around her heart. As the threat gets closer, can Logan protect Cassie and protect his heart? (Mature Adult, 18+)

Ragan's Song (Fairfield Corners Book 2) - It only took one look into his eyes for Ragan to know she was in trouble. Adam Bricklin has heard the melody in his head for years, the melody that told him if a decision was right or wrong. When he met Ragan Newlin, the song told him she was the one. Devastated when circumstances tore them apart, it has taken three years for him to finally move past the heartbreak. With a new girlfriend, a new album in the works, and his daughter doing well in school, things are looking bright; until the day Ragan returned to Fairfield Corners bearing secrets that could change their lives forever. (Mature, 18+)

Loving Jessie's Girl - Fiercely independent, Rina Abbot hid her true situation from everyone, including her best friend, Jessie. Out of money and unable to care for her rescue dogs she had no choice but to accept the help of the handsome stranger with a familiar face. Afraid to trust him, she tried to ignore the feelings he stirred within her as they searched for his missing brother...

Preacher's Redemption - With the past and the present on a collision course can their love survive?

2nd Chance Valentine - A chance encounter in a bar with the one who got away had Cam Beckett dreaming of his own happily ever after. But, only if he could convince Kara to forget their disastrous first date and give him a second chance.

My Grumpy Valentine - Ashley Sweet was living her dream—baking cupcakes and making plans to expand her bakery—until Thorton Hodges walked in with an offer she could, and did, refuse.

Hawk's Last First Kiss - Would Sadie be Hawk's last first kiss?

Christmas Grump - Stuck together in her tiny house, would the Grump ruin her holiday mood?

Quin to the Rescue - Rescuing her cat from a tree was only the beginning.

A Whisper Through Time - Will Jaya choose love or peace?

Heart of a Tin Man - Can the heart-hardened Tin Man save Dorrie and her little dog too?

Also from the Lavish Publishing family

SAMANTHA JACOBEY

Rendered (Irrevocable Series Book 1)
Samantha Jacobey
https://books2read.com/Rendered

The end of the world is coming, or so they say, and that puts Bailey Dewitt on a crash course with Armageddon. Orphaned, she and her young brothers find themselves living with their renegade uncle as part of a group of survivalists. She struggles against them, searching for a way to escape, but every discovery only terrifies her more.

For Caleb Cross, the Ranch is a way of life. The members of their group are family, and none should come between them. Smitten from the moment he met Bailey, his choices are no longer easy, his path no longer clear. He wants to welcome her and the twins into their fold and hopes his kin will agree.

But the elders who lead them aren't interested in the troublesome girl. They are plotting for the time they will be rid of her and expect Caleb to go along with their plans - he is after all one of them.

At first, Bailey resists Caleb's charms, but soon must admit that she desperately needs a friend. She has no intention of anything more, but when the elders make their move, she is forced to trust him with her very life.

They both have hard lessons to learn. Relationships built on secrets and lies don't come with guarantees. When the world falls apart around them, some things are Irrevocable.

Realistic sci-fi and romantic suspense will pull you into to the first book of the Irrevocable Trilogy.

Summer's Deceit (The Trilogy Book 1)
Sara J. Bernhardt
https://books2read.com/SummersDeceit

Jane Callahan is a reclusive, seventeen-year-old high school student dealing with the death of her beloved brother. Her home in Southern California with her mother is a constant reminder of her loss and pain. In hopes of escaping her past she moves to North Bend Oregon to live with her father, where she meets a beautiful boy named Aidan Summers.

Jane is intrigued by his looks as well as his unusual ways of attempting to get her attention. After months of uncommon conversation and frustration, an uncertain romance brews between Jane and Aidan, but Aidan has a ghastly secret that could destroy everything.

Get swept away by The Hunter's Trilogy – YA romantic suspense with a paranormal twist.